'This is the inspiring story of a
wounded in battle but also carrying
begins the long slow road to heal
Philip's journey from the battlef
greenness and peace of rural Wales,
he meets along the way all set against the vividly drawn background
of the natural world, the changing seasons and the gentle rhythms
of monastic life. I found Philip's story enthralling, well told and
the characters human and believable. A tale of forgiveness, hope,
renewed faith, and love.'
Eleanor Watkins, author

'This is an account of how kindness and grace are more powerful
than the sword; where Christian love reaches out to fight against
self-destruction. Joy bravely draws on her own experience of pain
and hopelessness in her journey back to health and strength of
body and spirit. Gentle, yet forceful, her story shows how love can
restore our hope and trust in both God and man.'
Alick Ford, retired teacher and Anglican lay reader

'Thirteenth century France and Wales form the backdrop to this
well-researched tale of a world-weary knight and his newly found
Cistercian friends. Interspersed with provocative and thought-
provoking Bible verses, we are carried into a world of peace, rest
and service, along with the constant worry of discovery and
betrayal. A feel-good exploration of forgotten times that leaves a
final lump in the throat.'
*Ian Hampson, Lay Reader, Church in Wales, and student of Welsh
ecclesiastical history*

'What a great book. An engaging story set in a realistic historical
context. If you thought living a life of faith was about following a
set of cold, joyless rules, have a read of this. Take a look at Philip's
life and journey with him out of the shadows into the radiance of
healing grace. Impossible to read without encountering hope.'
Billy Doey, Senior Pastor (Retired), Welcome Evangelical Church, Witney

The Healing

Joy Margetts

instant
ap□stle

First published in Great Britain in 2021

Instant Apostle
The Barn
1 Watford House Lane
Watford
Herts
WD17 1BJ

British Library Cataloguing-in-Publication Data

A catalogue record for this book is available from the British Library.

This book and all other Instant Apostle books are available from Instant Apostle:

Website: www.instantapostle.com

Email: info@instantapostle.com

ISBN 978-1-912726-42-4

Printed in Great Britain.

For Lynn, my friend
Who didn't give up on me even when I wanted to give up on myself, and who always spoke the truth with love.

For Keren, my daughter
Our rainbow of creativity. Who inherited my love for writing but was far braver than me. You made me do this.

For Peter, my son
Who shares my love of history, and reawakened my love for all things medieval.

For Tim, my husband
Who always loves me, always champions me, and always gives me space to be myself.

And for God
Thank You for giving me this book as a gift.
I give it back to You.

Contents

Author's note

This story came out of my own life experience, in combination with an insatiable appetite for history and a love of historic fiction. I too have experienced my own journey of healing and life restoration, and many of the lessons Hywel imparts to Philip are things that I have learned or had to relearn myself. I can point to many people who have been Hywel-type figures in my life, who stood by me in the darkest times and willed me to choose life, choose hope and choose to forgive. My thanks go to them, and this work is in part dedicated to them. But my greatest thanks goes to God who never left me, even when it felt like He had, and who has proved Himself to be exactly who He has promised to be in my life: My Healer, Provider, Sustainer, Refuge, Saviour and Redeemer.

For more information about the author and the story behind *The Healing*, visit joymargetts.com

Historical note

Philip de Braose was a real man but not much is known about him. Some of the people and events described in this book did actually happen, particularly those involving the de Braose family and their relationship to Llewellyn Fawr and the kings of England. Philip did have a tumultuous start to life. His father and grandmother were murdered by King John and his disgraced grandfather died in exile. Philip and his elder brother, John, spent much of their early years in captivity or in hiding. His brother did eventually regain his de Braose lands, including the Lordship of Gower. He also recovered a measure of favour with the change of English kings, and an advantageous Welsh marriage with Llewellyn's daughter. That is where the trail runs cold for the rest of the life of Philip de Braose. Nothing more is known about him. His brother John died young and his lands passed to his own son, William.

I stole Philip for my story as he fitted in well, especially with his family connections with Llewellyn Fawr (the Great), Prince of all Wales. I wanted to use Abbey Cymer as Hywel's home abbey as it is local to me and a place I love and know well. Llewellyn was also a patron of the Abbey, sourcing his horses from the breeding programme there, so there was the link I needed to make the story fit. I did what research I could on the Cistercian way of life in the period, but do not claim to be an expert in any way. Needless to say, my imagination is responsible for much of the rest of the historic content and character portrayals in this book. My apologies if I have corrupted or misrepresented people, places or customs in my attempts to add authenticity to my tale.

Route through Wales

N
↑

Abergwyngregyn

Dolwyddelan

Abbey Cymer

Map showing the
route through
wales

Staylittle

Abbey Cwmhir

Buellt

Talgarth

Grace Dieu

Swansea

Tintern Abbey

Gower

Chepstow

1
Awakening

Winter, early 1231
France

Philip became aware of a shuffling sound. It was pitch dark, and eerily quiet. Except for the shuffling. A mouse, or a rat maybe? He strained his ears, trying to hear the tell-tale sounds of claws scratching, at the same time lifting his hand up from where it had hung lifeless over the side of the bed. He didn't want to chance his fingers being nibbled. He had seen that before, rats nibbling at not-yet-dead men's fingers and toes, as they lay wounded on muddy battlefields. The shuffling stopped. Philip held his breath, and listened. Nothing. He allowed himself to relax and closed his eyes to welcome back the oblivion of sleep.

What was that now? More shuffling, a flash of bright light shining into his barely closed eyes, and a very human-sounding 'humph' as someone sat down heavily close to his head. Philip was wide awake now, but did not stir or open his eyes to betray his alert state. He didn't know where he was, or who his companion was, but he would not be taken unawares. He listened again. The man, whoever he was, was mumbling the same phrases over and over again. Was he in a prison cell with a madman?

He did not think he was chained. That was a bonus; it meant he could possibly make his escape. Keeping as still as possible, he reached out with his hand, the one hidden from the stranger by his own body, to feel for his sword belt. Gone. His knife? It had been tucked into the waistband of his linen braies.[1] He felt beneath himself. There was no knife, no waistband and no braies! So they had taken his clothes? He was naked apart from the rough woollen tunic he wore, and that was definitely not his own. And they had his weapons? He would have to rely on his hands alone, then, to fight. He was confident that would be enough. He was not big in height or build, but he was strong, agile and fit. He had faced enough in the thirty or so years since his birth to know his own ability when it came to fighting.

Philip waited for his moment. He needed to time it right. The figure beside him shifted, and mumbling done, he began to sing softly. Philip held his breath. Wait… Singing? Nothing made sense, except that the music the stranger's voice made was soul-stirringly beautiful. Perhaps he would just lie here and let the sound wash over him. He was so tired. Sleep beckoned and Philip felt himself relax. But as he relaxed he became aware of something else. A throbbing, gnawing pain in his left leg. He tried to quietly shift position to ease it, bending his knee slightly.

'Argh!'

It took him a moment to realise it was he that had screamed out in agony. He tried to sit up to grab his knee, but moving his head produced a searing pain of its own, and he fell back onto the bed, sweating profusely. He was then aware of the gentle weight of a hand on his right shoulder.

'Lie still, my friend, and the pain will become bearable again.' The voice was low and musical, the touch reassuring, not threatening. Philip opened his eyes but could not focus through the pain and dim light. A face loomed and a hand holding a flickering candle hovered above his head.

'There, now. It is good to see you awake, but I warrant you would rather not be. I will get you a draft to help you sleep again.'

---

[1] Trouser-like undergarments, tied at the waist.

'Where am I? Who are you? What happened to me?' Philip forced the questions through parched lips, his voice raspy and unrecognisable as his own. He was willing the throbbing in his head to stop. He needed to be able to think clearly.

'All in good time, all in good time. Suffice it to say that you are safe here. In our hands and in God's. I am Brother Clement, and you need to rest and recover. That is all you need to know for now... Here, can you take this?' A hand snaked gently around behind his head, easing it up, and he felt the rim of a cup against his lips.

Could he trust this monk? He had met so-called holy men before who would not hesitate to poison a helpless man for their own ends. But did he have a choice? Death itself might be better than this agony. He opened his lips and drank. The draft was bitter, but sweetened with honey. He had drunk worse. Another cup followed, and he took a gulp of cool, clear water that soothed his parched throat and dry lips.

'Lie back and let sleep take you. I will keep my vigil at your side. I'll try not to disturb you again with my psalmody.'

Philip let himself be lowered back down. 'It was the music of heaven,' he sighed, as sleep overcame him again.

When Philip became aware of his surroundings again, the sun had risen; light was streaming through a small window, high above him. Trying not to move his head too much, he scanned his surroundings to get a picture of where he was. He could see wooden roof beams above him, and stone walls on two sides at least. Another high window opposite revealed a blue sky with small white clouds. Not an underground dungeon, then. He used his hands to decipher that he was lying on a simple bed of wooden sides, with rope stringing and a straw-filled mattress. It smelled clean. And he was covered with a clean blanket. His arms and legs were unshackled. So it was likely that he was not in a prison of any kind. He could hear sounds coming from outside, a cock crowing, hens clucking, a blackbird singing, and in the distance voices singing chant-like. Ah yes... It was beginning to make more sense. A man calling himself a brother had tended to him in the night. Clement… Was it? He was in a holy house of some sort. But where, exactly? And how had he got here? And why was he in such abominable pain? He needed answers, he needed more water, and he needed to… relieve himself. He groaned at the thought. His stomach grumbled. He needed food too.

'Water, please. Is anyone there?' It came out as a harsh whisper.

Nothing. He gingerly tried lifting his head a bit more; the pain was still there, but bearable. There was an empty stool and a small table alongside his bed, with the remains of a burned-out candle, and a cup. Philip tried to twist to reach his hand towards the cup. No! The searing pain as he tried to bend his left knee ripped through him, and he fell back onto the bed, breathing heavily.

'There now, young man. Let me get that for you.'

A small figure dressed all in white, with a matching tonsured head of snow-white hair, bustled in. Philip recognised the kind voice from the night before and closed his eyes with relief. He hated being dependent on anyone, but as he drank thirstily from the cup proffered to his lips he was most grateful for the monk's assistance.

'Thank you.' It sounded a bit more like his own voice now.

'You are most welcome.' The age-worn face smiled back at him. 'We are pleased you decided to come back to us.'

'Come back? Where have I been?'

'My guess, my friend, is that you have likely been to hell and back. In your dreams, at least.'

Philip was still trying to think clearly. 'Forgive me, I am struggling to understand.'

'Do not worry yourself. There is time for making sense of the past, and time for planning for the future, but this is not that time. This is the present, and here we must attend to your needs as they are. Some food perhaps, and some water to wash yourself?'

'I need to…' Philip felt his face flush.

'Of course,' Clement smiled knowingly. 'We can see to that also.'

Some time later, Philip lay back on the bed, exhausted. Clement had returned with a tall, broad, slightly younger-looking monk with laughing eyes. A little broth had eased the rumbling in his stomach, and another different-tasting draft had eased the pain as they ministered to his needs. Those ministrations included the cleansing and redressing of a wound above his left knee that Philip could not see but could definitely feel. The worst pain, however, was his left knee itself. He would ask about that in due time. The monks worked mostly in silence, nodding to one another more than speaking.

'How long was I asleep?' Philip broke the peace.

Brother Clement was rinsing the soiled dressings in a pail of clean water, his habit sleeves turned up to his elbows. 'Well, now, that is a good question! We cannot be exactly sure but I would guess at least six days and nights, possibly more. Brother Hywel here brought you to our door five days ago, and you were definitely not awake then.' He laughed a small laugh and smiled over at the other monk, who grinned back at him.

That long. 'I was injured in a fight?'

'It seems so. It was definitely a weapon of some sort made that dent in your head.' Philip's hand crept unbidden to the lump above his left ear. 'That's what most likely put you to sleep, although the fever that followed the wounding…' he nodded towards Philip's leg wound, '… is certainly what kept you asleep. You did not sleep peacefully, though. You fought many battles. At times both of us had to hold you still. You called out many names as well, and swore a time or two!'

The other monk had come to stand by his bedside, his hands on his hips. What had Clement called him? Hywel? A Welsh name. A momentary twinge of longing ran through Philip. Hywel was smiling.

'Less said the better about those profanities you uttered. One or two of the brothers were shocked by what they heard coming from this room in the middle of the night.'

'My knee?' Philip turned his face slightly to ask Hywel the question. The monk's face grew more serious.

'We are concerned that the same weapon that split the skin above your knee also split your knee. That is why it hurts so to bend it.'

Philip took in this information, unsure as to what it would mean. 'Will it mend?'

'I believe so.' Clement walked over to join them. 'I have seen broken bones mend plenty of times, with rest and the right exercise. And now that the fever has passed, you stand a better chance of full recovery.'

'I would trust what he says,' laughed Hywel. 'He is the infirmarer here. I am more a horse man myself. Give me a strained fetlock any day!'

Clement continued, 'Your leg may not be as it was. But I am certain that you will be able to walk on it again, at least. You are young enough and strong enough, but you still have some recovery to fight for. At least now you can use your energy to fight the right battle, eh? Not the one in your dreams. And now I fear you must rest again.' Clement pulled the light bed-covering up to Philip's waist and nodded at Hywel. They both turned to leave.

'You said before that you believe I went to hell and back?'

Clement paused and turned back to face Philip. 'You were obviously in torment in your dreams and memories. You begged to die. You begged to die more than once, but we prayed that you would live. That you would *choose* to live. Every time you cried out in anguish in your dreams, every time it looked like you were fading away from us, I willed you to live. I whispered to you, "Choose life, choose life."'

'Why?' Philip was still struggling to make sense of it all, his head fuzzy with exhaustion and the effects of whatever draft they had given him.

'Because, my child, God's will is for you to live. Your life can have meaning and purpose. There is always hope while there is life. But you have to choose. To live, and to hope. Choose hope, and I have every belief that you will not regret the life God leads you into.'

Philip had closed his eyes and was breathing evenly.

Clement was not even sure that Philip had heard all that he had said to him. He smiled sadly to himself. 'And so the battle begins,' he whispered, 'but at least you are alive to fight it now.' Clement stood watching the sleeping man for a moment longer. 'I have hope that you can win the battle for the recovery of your body,' he said, softly. 'The recovery of your mind, soul and spirit – that I am still not sure of. That is another battle that only you can choose to fight.'

'Come, brother,' Hywel had paused in the doorway. 'He needs our prayers now more than he needs our presence.'

Philip rode pell-mell into the fight. The horse beneath him was puffing and blowing, but Philip didn't care about Noble's exhaustion. Philip didn't care about anything. His sword was raised above his head and he let out a great roar. If he was going to die, he was going to take at least one other with him. He was surrounded on all sides, but he would not go down without a fight. He welcomed death. He had had enough of life. Every fight they now faced, he made sure he was in the thick of it, hoping that an unseen blade or well-placed arrow would take him down before he realised it. Faced with a blade, instinct took over and Philip would fight to defend himself. He needed someone to take him out when he was not ready for them, or for a stray arrow to hit him in the neck. All around were heaving bodies, the sickening smell of blood, the clang of steel, the whinnying of terrified horses and the screams of dying men – blood-curdling screams. Sweat poured down Philip's back and he swung his sword at the head of an approaching rider, making contact with his raised shield. He reached to grab the shield out of the way so that he could make his final thrust into his opponent's face. He felt the rage rise up within him, the bloodlust, mixed with sheer terror. Noble stumbled slightly beneath him and Philip lost his hold on the rider's shield. He used his leg strength to steady himself, and raised his sword arm again to strike, but as he did so the shield he had just lost hold of came hurtling towards his head, stunning him. As he slumped forward half-conscious in the saddle, he was aware of a sudden excruciating pain as the full weight of a broad sword made contact with his left leg. And then nothing. Blackness.

He was suddenly aware of the weight of something on his shoulder. Philip tensed again and furiously tried to free himself, but he could not move.

'Wake up, my boy. You need to wake up.' A firm voice. A flickering light shone in Philip's face. He was being shaken gently by the shoulder. Philip opened his eyes slowly. His breathing was coming fast and shallow, and he was clutching the bed covers beneath him. Sweat trickled down between his shoulder blades and his forehead was drenched.

'Lie still, now. Slow your breathing down. Relax. You are safe here.' The voice came from just above him to the right. He turned to try to focus on where it was coming from. A dark, greying tonsure above a sun-weathered face, and concerned eyes framed with laughter lines. Hywel. He closed his eyes and relaxed his hands. His breathing slowed as he willed himself back to the present.

'I was dreaming,' he said hoarsely.

'I guessed as much, by the way you screamed out. It made me come running, thinking you had tried to get out of bed again, only to find you thrashing about, fighting with your sheets.' Hywel's tone was light, and he held humour in his voice, but his eyes remained concerned. 'You had many a dream like that one when you were in the throes of fever, and we couldn't wake you then. I thought it best to bring you back to the present this time. You need your energy now for the real fights, not the imaginary ones,' he continued, as he passed Philip a cup of water and handed him a clean cloth to wipe his face.

'It was so real. A memory. It must have been the last fight, when I was wounded. I remember now how it happened.' Philip shuddered, and his hand moved instinctively to touch his healing leg wound.

Hywel sat on the stool by Philip's bed and put the candle on the table beside him, stretching his long legs out. His head was bowed and his hands folded in his lap. Is he waiting for my confession? Philip thought to himself. The older man certainly didn't look in any hurry to leave him.

'Do you know who I am?' Philip broke the silence.

'Do *you* know who you are?' Hywel laughed quietly in response. 'We weren't sure if you would remember, with that blow to your head.'

Philip grimaced. 'I am Philip de Braose,' he announced, pausing to see what effect it had on the monk.

Hywel did not respond at all.

'You know the de Braose name?' Philip tried another tack.

Hywel looked up at him and sighed. 'Every Welshman, most Englishmen and a fair number of the French know the de Braose name – and many fear it,' he added as an aside. 'So I can call you Philip, that is useful to know.' He kept his tone light, as before.

Philip snorted. 'Yes, that would be preferable to "boy", at least.'

'So I am right in assuming this last fight was not your first? You would have been trained to fight, carrying a name of such notoriety.'

'I am a soldier. I have fought all over France. At first I fought for a cause I thought I believed in. But more recently I have fought for coin in my purse and for...' Philip paused.

'A longing for death?' Hywel finished the thought for him.

'Yes. I have seen so much, endured so much, been painfully betrayed. I have grown weary of this life and its cruelties. That

23

last fight… I went into it wishing for it to be my last ever. For the misery of my life to be ended.'

'We had guessed as much.' Hywel spoke gently. 'It seems God had other plans for you, though.'

Philip did not respond to that. He closed his eyes again and there was silence. He felt Hywel's hand rest on his upper arm, squeezing it reassuringly.

After some minutes had passed, Philip spoke again. 'How did I get here? I remember nothing after the blow… The pain.'

'I found you. Rather, I found your horse. And I can never pass a good-looking horse by,' Hywel laughed quietly. 'He was standing by the roadside, complete with saddle and tack, but no rider. I went over to him, and he led me to you. You were lying seemingly dead in a ditch. I assume your horse had ridden from the fight, and somehow, God only knows how, you had managed to stay on his back long enough until he deposited you where I found you. I quickly surmised you were not dead, and managed to heave you back up onto the back of your poor horse – who took the indignity well, I must say. I led you both here. The rest you know.'

'My horse. He is here?' Philip gingerly lifted himself up onto his elbows. Hywel's answer to that particular question was important to him.

'Yes. He is here, enjoying himself in the stables in the company of the two mares I have just purchased. He is well fed and well rested. You do not need to worry about him.'

'Noble,' Philip breathed out, as he relaxed back down on to the bed.

'Oh, is that his name? Suits him. He is a proud and somewhat stubborn old man!'

Philip closed his eyes. He needed to sleep again. 'I will tell you more, I promise. You deserve that much.'

'When you can, and not before. Sleep easy now, Philip. And God rest your troubled soul.'

I have come that they may have life,

and that they may have it more abundantly.

John 10:10, NKJV

2
Despair

The days seemed to drag by. Philip wished sometimes that he could go back to the oblivion of the days of fever-fuelled semiconsciousness. Now every day was an endless cycle of routines that he had no control over. He was still dependent on the monks to care for him. The wound above his knee was more or less healed, and his head felt a great deal more normal, but his knee was still painful and swollen, and limited his movement considerably. He could half-sit up in the bed, to wash his face and feed himself, but was dependent on the brothers for most other things. He was beyond frustrated.

The bells that rang to announce the prayer offices dictated his days. The monks flitted between the church and the infirmary, with his wash water, dressings, food and drink. When they had finished with him, sometimes they would stay for a while, but as talking above the necessary was forbidden within the rules of their Order, Philip began to resent even their silent presence. When he was left alone, though, his own thoughts did him even less good. The demons were very real inside his own head, as real as the holy brothers singing their psalms in the nearby church. Sometimes Philip would try to quieten the noise in his head and concentrate on listening to the melodic music, but before long his thoughts would take him down darker paths again.

To encourage his knee to recover, Clement had devised a set of exercises for it, and he and Hywel took turns in bullying

Philip into doing them. The pain and sheer effort exhausted him, and he resented them insisting on his compliance. Much as he wanted to use his leg, walk again, ride again, Philip's initial motivation had waned when it seemed to be such a slow and painful process, with so little obvious progress. A fortnight had passed and he was still in this bed, still an invalid. Still dependent on others, imprisoned by his own body and the infirmary walls. It was a comfortable enough prison, but it was still a prison to him. Occasionally he had been joined by another patient – an old man with an irritating cough, or a fat monk who snored loudly all night and wheezed loudly all day – but thankfully, for the most part, Philip had been on his own. He was not good company for anyone anyway.

Hywel appeared at Philip's bedside with a determined look on his face, interrupting his musings.

'Something different today, I think. Raise yourself up, Philip. We are going to see if we can get you sitting up on the side of the bed.'

'*What?* I can't yet bend the knee fully and you want me to put myself through the agony of having to bend it over the side of the bed?' Philip growled in response.

'Complain all you want, young man, but if you want to ever walk on that leg, we have to try this.'

He reached over to put his arm under Philip's upper arm, half-forcing, half-helping him to sit upright in the bed.

'Right, keep hold of my arm as you twist around towards me. Move your good leg first and then the left leg slowly and carefully.' Hywel took control of the manoeuvre.

Philip concentrated on making his leg muscles do what he willed them to do, using Hywel's strength to steady himself. As his right leg found its way over the side of the bed, Hywel let go of Philip's arm and reached out to help support his left leg, taking it by the ankle, as Philip slowly swung himself around to perch on the edge of the bed. His right leg easily made contact with the stone floor, but his left leg was still more straight than bent, the weight of it resting in Hywel's hands.

'Now slowly bend this knee,' Hywel instructed, nodding at the offending limb.

Philip willed his leg to comply, and fighting the pain, he began to bend his knee, trying to match it to the healthy right leg. He bit his tongue to stop the oath that threatened to leave his lips. Why was it so difficult? The sweat was pouring off Philip as he concentrated on working through the pain. All at once it was all too much, his hands that had been supporting him behind gave way and Philip fell back on the bed with a thud, his leg screaming in agony. He closed his eyes, his face contorted.

Hywel carefully repositioned Philip's legs back on the bed, and gave him a moment to compose himself.

'We'll try again tomorrow,' he said quietly.

'*We* will, will we? I really don't see how it is going to be any better tomorrow. It is hopeless. Waste of my effort and your time! Why don't you just leave me alone?' Frustration gave way to full-blown rage and Philip barely contained the profanities he would have loved to have used.

Hywel stood, quietly tucking his hands into the sleeves of his habit and lowering his head slightly, apparently waiting for the storm to pass. He was right to wait. As quickly as Philip's rage had erupted, it died, followed by an overwhelming sense of hopelessness.

'I am so sick of this life. I see no purpose to my existence. I am a burden to you all, and I want it all to be over.'

Philip turned his head to the wall, covering it with his arm. His whole body shuddered. It was grief, but he would not let it out. He didn't cry. He didn't feel. He had trained himself not to feel. It was just all so empty, so meaningless. He was done fighting, he was too tired to fight. He let the despair wash over him.

After some moments he heard Hywel's voice speaking gently.

'God led me to you, Philip, in that roadside ditch, for a purpose. You would have surely died within hours if you had laid there undiscovered, and many who passed by would as soon have stolen your horse and left you to die than gone out of their way to help a wounded soldier. God sent me along that road on the right day, and at the right time, and I brought you here. Clement and I tended you, and we prayed over you, and willed you to live, because we believed that was what God's will was for you. And then you awoke and we knew the first battle, for life itself, was won, but that there would be many more battles to come for you. Some little skirmishes, like trying to bend your knee over the side of the bed here, some full-blown battles, like the one you are fighting with despair just at this moment. We willed you to choose life, and you did. Now, Philip, I am urging you to choose hope. You can let the despair take you, or you can choose another way.'

'How?' It was a one-word muffled response, forced out from where he lay, his face still covered.

'I know it seems an impossibility to you, that there could be something better for you than this life here and now. Or a life better than your life that has passed before. But surely choosing to believe there could be is better than believing that there definitely isn't...' Hywel paused for a few moments before asking, 'Have you faith in God?'

'I did have once.'

'Then there is definitely hope for you.' The bell for Vespers was ringing to call the brothers to prayer. 'I will leave you now, but I have one other thing for you to think on, Philip. Being thankful is a good place to start in order to begin to see things more positively. Be thankful for the everyday things, big and small. Focus your mind on those good things that you are grateful for.'

'What exactly have I got to be grateful for?' Philip rolled over onto his back and challenged Hywel with a look.

'You'll see, soon enough,' he said, as he turned away, chuckling to himself.

Philip could time things by the ringing of those bells. He knew after Vespers that one of the monks would be back with some bread and warm ale for his supper, before they returned to the church for Compline, and then to bed. They retired as soon as the sun went down during these colder months, and the dark hours stretched long for Philip, when sleep did not come. Sometimes they would offer him a draft to help him sleep, but he usually refused. Sometimes they would leave him a candle, and Hywel had brought him a beautifully illustrated Psalter to look at. He had taken to reading a psalm some nights by the flickering candlelight. He could relate to some of those psalms; it seemed the writer wasn't a stranger to grief, pain, betrayal or despair himself. Morning would come with the sun, although the monks would have been called from their beds in the early hours for Vigils. They would call in after Lauds at daybreak with his breakfast, which was always the same: fresh bread, a small piece of cheese and a cup of warmed goat's milk. Later in the morning Clement would appear with his wash water and clean linens, and then, before going for his own midday meal, the monk would make sure Philip had his. Every day it was a pottage made with grains, vegetables and herbs; simple food, but warm and filling.

That evening it was Hywel who returned to him with his supper. The monk came in silently and put a plate and cup down on the table next to Philip's bed.

'Eat up,' he nodded to the plate.

Philip reached over to take it. Just a few crumbs of stale bread! He picked up the cup and took a sip, anticipating the warming ale. Water. And freezing cold water at that.

'What, no thanks?' Hywel asked quizzically.

Philip grimaced. Point well made, Hywel, he thought to himself. But he played along.

'My thanks for my supper, brother,' he replied sarcastically.

'Sleep well, then,' Hywel turned to leave him.

'Have you no candle for me tonight?' Philip looked up from contemplating whether to force the dry crumbs of bread down his throat, or to leave them for the mice.

'Candle? No candle tonight.' Hywel paused but did not turn.

'But... ah. Well played again, brother. *I would be most grateful,*' Philip emphasised the words, 'for the use of a candle to read the Scriptures by tonight.'

'What, thankful that I have provided you with both candle and manuscript for all these past few nights?'

Hywel did turn at this, and looked pointedly at Philip, trying to hold back a grin.

'Yes, brother,' Philip sighed. 'I submit. I am grateful. And for the delicious supper you have brought me every night.'

Hywel bowed dramatically and turned again to leave, returning a few moments later with a lit candle, a slice of fresh bread and a beaker of ale.

Hywel's little game continued well into the next day, when the goat's milk came sour at breakfast, and the pottage cold at lunchtime. Clement was in on it also. The wash water he brought to Philip was a little dribble in the bottom of the basin, and the monk seemingly 'forgot' Philip's clean linens. By the afternoon Philip was ready to concede. There was much he could complain about maybe, but much that he could also be genuinely grateful for. The little things, certainly. He just had to decide which he would focus on, the not-so-good things or the good things.

Hywel had another surprise for him after dinner. He appeared with a contraption that looked suspiciously like a fine dining chair, probably borrowed from the abbot's dining room, only it had wheels, not legs – two at the front and a third behind. Hywel wheeled it over to the side of Philip's bed and then disappeared again, returning with a plank of wood.

'I wanted to see if you could sit with your knee bent yesterday, because I wanted to see if you could sit in this.' He pointed to the chair. 'I think you need a change of scene from this room that you have begun to consider little more than a prison cell.' He looked knowingly at Philip, who felt himself blush.

'It is a fine day,' he continued. 'Chilly in the shade, but the sun is bright and warm, and I think a few moments outside in the fresh air would do you the world of good. And help with your frame of mind,' he added, the last words under his breath.

'Chilly? It was snowing yesterday!' Philip definitely wasn't sure about this, and could feel a slight sense of panic at the thought.

'A lot of things were different yesterday,' Hywel said, looking directly at him. 'Today the snow is gone and the sun is warming the earth; the birds are singing and creation is expectant of spring approaching. We celebrate the present and the blessings of each day.' Point made, he turned his attention to the matter in hand. 'Come, let's see if we can get you into this thing. I have brought this plank to put under your knee to keep your leg straight, if it is more comfortable for you.'

Philip stared at the wheeled chair. He was very reluctant to move, knowing it would be painful, and exhausting, but he had to admit that getting out of the infirmary was extremely appealing. And someone had gone to the trouble of making this chair for him; one of the lay brothers, most probably. He didn't want to appear ungrateful. He smiled slightly to himself. Could he be learning the lesson of thankfulness already?

With a combined effort, Hywel lifting him more than Philip moving himself, they got him into the chair, with the wooden plank fitted under him to support his left leg.

'Now let's see if this thing moves with the weight of you in it.'

'You mean, you don't know if it is even going to work?' Philip was sweating and puffing with the effort he had made to get into the chair, and he let his frustration show momentarily, before quickly realising Hywel was teasing him again.

Hywel was grinning broadly as he turned the chair around with ease and pushed Philip towards the open doors of the infirmary. The other side of the door led to a small corridor that went both ways. One way led to the enclosed cloister and the Abbey buildings, the other way to a walled herb garden. Hywel turned the chair in the direction of the garden and in a few steps they were outside in the cool air. The sky was a pale blue with a few stringy white clouds and the high winter sun was doing its very best to try to warm things up.

A small, wiry monk with a dark tonsure and leathered face glanced up from his work and nodded at Hywel. 'Brother Francis,' Hywel whispered into Philip's ear. 'Loves plants more than people, but is a kind enough soul. He won't mind us being here while he works.'

Philip closed his eyes and took a deep breath of the cool, slightly herb-scented air. He felt the gentle warmth of the sun touch his face and turned it in order to get the full benefit of the sunlight. It did feel good. It felt *very* good. In a way, it made him feel more alive. The sun, the fresh air, the birdsong, the scents and sounds. Deep within him something stirred to life, as his senses drank in his surroundings.

Hywel pushed him a little further down the path towards an opening in the far wall. He stopped in a sunny spot, sheltered from the cool breeze, where Philip could see both the herb garden and the more open aspect beyond the walls. From what he could see, outside the walls looked like a small orchard, and beyond that, fields, brown and bare, but obviously used for cultivation. The herb garden was lovely, even in its winter state, and Philip could only imagine what it would be like in the spring and summer, with its scents and colours, but his eyes were drawn longingly to the open spaces beyond the walls. Freedom. But freedom from what? And for what? Not the life he had been living. Philip's thoughts suddenly threatened to take him down dark paths again and he willed himself back to the present, to what his senses were experiencing and how grateful that made him feel, right in the moment.

'See that tree over there?' Hywel's voice broke into his reverie. He was pointing out a large, bare apple tree. 'It looks dead.'

'Is it?' Philip asked. He didn't think it was dead, but he was no expert.

'Well, it looks dead. But I suppose looks can be deceiving.' Hywel spoke, seemingly all matter of fact.

'Why do you think it looks dead?' Philip wasn't at all sure where this was going, but he was curious.

'Well, its branches are bare. It has no green leaves, no white blossom, and definitely no apples, so it must be dead.'

'It is winter.' Philip didn't want to call the older monk a fool out of respect, but he couldn't quite conceive how the monk was speaking such nonsense. He studied Hywel's face, looking for clues.

'But it is an apple tree. It is supposed to bear apples,' Hywel continued, regardless of Philip's hard stare.

'Not in this season,' Philip said, with a hint of frustration.

Hywel glanced back at him, and smiled broadly. 'Ah. There you have it! It is not dead, we know it is not dead. It is just being shaped by the season it is in.' He continued, 'In the late summer these apple trees provide us with a bounty of fruit, but then as winter approaches their leaves turn brown and fall to the earth. But the tree does not die. It spends the winter months drawing water and nutrients from beneath the earth, via its root system, to make sure that it has all that it needs for the spring. In the spring, new leaf buds appear, and then in time blossom will follow, and finally in the right season fruit will come again.' Hywel paused.

'So even when things, when people, appear to be useless, lifeless, fruitless, it might not actually be that way. It might just be the season of life they are in.' Philip was thinking it through.

'Yes, Philip,' Hywel continued. 'The tree will bear fruit again. We have seen it so many times before to know that it is true. Spring always follows winter. While the tree lives, even through the winter, then there is hope that it will flourish again when spring comes. So it is with us. We are sometimes defined, and altered, by the hard things that life throws at us, but we can learn to even appreciate the winter seasons. It is often in those hard times that God is doing the deepest and most important things inside us, to prepare us for the more fruitful seasons of our lives that will inevitably follow. Our responsibility is to make sure our roots are deep and grounded in truth. In God, and what He says.'

Philip thought quietly for a few moments. He wasn't sure he got it fully yet but he could see there was truth in what Hywel had said. 'Thank you,' he said, 'and I mean that genuinely.' He smiled slightly at the monk.

'For what, Philip?' Hywel was pushing him to voice it.

'For everything. For this,' he thumped the chair arm, 'and this,' he gestured around him, taking in all the signs of new life he could see beginning to appear. 'And for being such a wise old man,' he said, with a small smile.

'Not so much of the old, if you don't mind, but I'll take the wise. And I'll thank God for that!' Hywel smiled back.

'You've given me much to ponder.' Philip shivered slightly. The thick woollen cloak that Hywel had put around Philip's shoulders was no longer keeping out the chill.

'Can you cope with being outside for just a few minutes more? There is something else I really want to show you.'

'As long as we are quick,' Philip replied. The discomfort in his leg was beginning to mar the pleasure of the experience for him now.

Hywel disappeared through the opening in the wall and out of Philip's sight. In barely a few minutes he was back, but he wasn't alone. In his hands he held some reins, and looming proudly beside him was the bulk of a huge, dark horse.

Noble! If he could have leapt out of the chair Philip would have done, the moment of sheer joy was so intense. The great horse stepped up and dipped his head into Philip's chest, snickering gently. Philip felt his eyes tearing up. This was too much. He could barely contain the emotion. To cry over a horse! Ridiculous. But this was how it felt to feel again. The joy was real and it shocked him to the core that he could feel it so intensely. He reached up and stroked the familiar muzzle, and tickled Noble's ears, and then buried his head in the horse's neck, holding tightly to his mane.

Hywel stood by, watching as man and horse reconnected. The horse seemed to know instinctively what to do. Hywel gave them some moments together before stepping up and taking hold of Noble's reins again.

'I must take him from you, I'm afraid. The lay brother there,' he nodded to someone just out of Philip's sightline, 'is waiting to take him back to the stables for me. And you are getting too cold to be outside much longer. I will bring him to see you again, or else take you to see him. And before you know it, you will be walking him, and tending him, and riding him again yourself.'

'I hope that I will,' Philip said, as he let Hywel take the horse from him, and he meant it. It was not wishful thinking. He felt a determination rising within him to make those things happen.

'And hope is good,' Hywel replied, with a knowing smile.

For I know the thoughts that I think toward you, says

the LORD,

thoughts of peace and not of evil, to give you a future

and a hope.

Jeremiah 29:11, NKJV

3
Peas

The nights were getting shorter and the days warmer by the time Philip could be totally rid of that wheeled chair. Not that he was ungrateful for it. It had enabled him to continue getting outside, when the weather permitted. On one or two occasions, Hywel had even managed the long trek around to the stables, swerving Philip's chair around muddy puddles and rattling over stony pathways.

Philip was more confident now that he would be able to handle walking Noble, maybe even riding him before too long. He had recovered much more movement in his left knee; it almost bent at right angles now, and he could walk on it, gingerly, and with the help of a rough-hewn crutch. He couldn't go far yet, and he was still easily exhausted, but it was definite progress.

The other battle, for peace of mind, was a longer fight, and Philip wasn't so sure of his progress on that front. There were still days when feelings of despair and hopelessness washed over him, and it was a battle to focus his mind on positive things, especially on the days when the weather kept him inside the four walls of the infirmary. He was trying to practise thankfulness, not always successfully. On days when he forgot to be thankful, or got frustrated with the ministering attention of the monks, he would inevitably catch Hywel's eye, have a flashback to the taste of sour goat's milk, and sheepishly apologise for his poor attitude.

Hywel had become his close companion. Clement was all gentleness, and always kind in his ministrations, but Hywel was a pleasure to be with. He was never far from laughter, and would tease and cajole, and brush off Philip's moans. Both brothers were wise, and able to dispense that wisdom, but Philip sensed in Hywel a deep understanding born out of his own life experience. He spoke to Philip as if he knew exactly what he was thinking and feeling, and his stories and analogies hit the mark in a way that the simply spoken words of truth that Clement offered didn't quite manage. And, of course, they had the love of horses in common.

Philip was finding moments of peace. He found it hard, inside the walls of the infirmary, to silence the fears and forget the tormenting memories, especially when alone at night. But outside, that was different. Now that he could walk a short distance, on fine days he would hobble out to the herb garden, where there was a useful bench set against the infirmary wall. Here he could deposit himself and rest from his exertions. By the afternoon, the early spring sun would shine directly on the spot where he sat. He could close his eyes, soaking in the warmth on his face, and breathe deeply. If he focused on the birds singing and chirping, or on the sound of Brother Francis digging or pulling weeds, then the sounds in his head would gradually diminish and a fragile peace would descend. Some days, when he had finished with his work, Hywel would come and sit by him. They would not speak, but sit in quiet companionship. Hywel called it 'contemplation time'. Philip suspected he was more often than not contemplating the inside of his eyelids, and a small snore would sometimes escape the monk's mouth.

On one particular day, Philip was watching Brother Francis digging soil drills along a portion of one of the side walls. Francis never spoke to him, even when the rules of the Order permitted it, but he carried his own quiet peace, and his care of the garden revealed his gentle heart. Philip would watch as he would often intentionally drop seed on the pathway behind him and as the birds would fearlessly gather to feast on it, unthreatened by Francis' presence. He was taking after his namesake, St Francis of Assisi, Philip smiled to himself when he saw it. And the monk didn't seem to mind Philip's presence in the garden either. On this afternoon Hywel had arrived puffing slightly, supposedly to help Francis with his digging. Seemingly the other monk was not too keen on Hywel's 'help', so he had come instead to sit by Philip.

'Peas,' he said as he sat down.

'Peas? Or peace?' Philip responded with a half-smile, not minding Hywel's intrusion in the least.

'Well, both, I suppose, but I was referring to our brother over there,' Hywel laughed, nodding over to where Francis was bent over the soil. 'He does carry peace, but he is also carrying peas.'

'Oh, the seed drills are for peas.'

'Yes.' Hywel rose again and sauntered over to Francis. He said nothing to the other monk but made some signs and then sauntered back to Philip, some dried-up, shrivelled peas in his hand.

'Don't look very promising, do they?' he said. 'Not tasty like this, either.' He put a dried pea between his teeth and demonstrated just how inedible they were. 'But I am assured, by one who knows these things, that these dried-up peas have the potential to grow into tall, healthy pea plants bearing lots of fresh green pea pods. Each of these single dried peas has the potential to produce a great number of fresh peas.'

'I can feel another lesson coming,' Philip groaned, good-naturedly.

'Some things don't really come to full life and fruitfulness until they are buried.'

Hywel made the short statement and then sat down again, absent-mindedly playing with the peas in his hand.

Philip waited. Was he going to say more? Or was he supposed to take something profound from that statement alone? A few minutes passed. When nothing more was said, Philip leaned back against the wall and closed his eyes. Peas? He'd happily just take peace at this moment.

'Do you know what month it is?'

Philip opened his eyes and looked at the back of Hywel's head. That was an unexpected question, but he wasn't so cut off from the real world that he had lost complete track of the changing of the months.

'It's March, I believe, and April is approaching.'

'So is Easter.'

'I suppose it must be.'

'Easter is a big event here.' Hywel nodded back towards the Abbey buildings. 'The Abbey church is open to the local people and it is a busy but joyous occasion, with lots of services and celebrations.'

What had Easter to do with peas? Those certainly wouldn't be grown and ready in time for the Easter celebrations. Was the monk talking nonsense again? But then, Philip remembered, the last time he had thought Hywel was speaking nonsense, it had made complete sense eventually.

'In the week before His death, Jesus talked about one seed having to be buried in order to bring new life to many. Only He used grain in his example, not peas,' Hywel said, after a while.

Ah, so there was a link. Tenuous, but a link.

'Well, that makes sense, because Jesus died and was buried in a tomb, but came back to life.' Philip knew the story well enough.

'Yes, and His resurrection life has given life to many. To all who believe in Him.' Hywel paused again for a few minutes before going on, 'I think that there is another lesson we can learn from these peas.'

Philip braced himself.

'You remember the dead apple tree that wasn't dead?'

Yes, Philip remembered; that was the other time he thought Hywel had lost his senses. He nodded.

'Well, in a similar way, these seemingly dead peas have extraordinary life-giving potential. Within each of these peas is all that is needed to create a healthy, fruit-bearing pea plant. They have to be buried, watered and tended, but they will produce life from what seems to be dried up and dead. Incredible, really.' He was now examining the peas closely in his hand.

'So, we can apply that to ourselves, can we?' Philip sighed. He wasn't sure where this was going, but Hywel had him intrigued.

'When I took my vows and entered the Order, I had to bury an old life. I had to put to death, if you like, my old desires and ambitions, and ways of behaviour. It wasn't easy, I can tell you, but I was finally able to do it. God honoured that, and I believe my life has become much more meaningful and fruitful as a result.'

'So you think I should do likewise, bury my old life by entering the Order?' Philip wasn't sure he wanted the answer to that question.

'No, no. Not necessarily.' Hywel paused, thoughtfully. 'I do think, however, that God brought you here to the Abbey, and into our care, for a reason. I think that He is giving you the opportunity to put to death – to bury, if you like – your old way of living. I believe if you do that and choose to follow His ways, your life can be more productive and fulfilling than you could ever imagine.'

'Any life would be better than the one I had been living.' Philip was sure of that one thing. There was no going back for him. He'd rather have died in that ditch than go back to his old life.

'I've no doubt of that. You also carry many burdens from that old life. In time you will have to learn to put them down, bury them also.'

Philip pondered this. Was it possible to actually be free of his old life, and the memories, the ones that came rushing back laden with guilt, pain, fear and anger? He couldn't see how that could be possible, but it was nice to think, sitting here, hidden away from the world, just him, a smiling monk and a pea planter, that life could perhaps be different. More peaceful, even. It was a pleasing thought.

'Perhaps as Easter approaches you will think some more on these things?' Hywel said.

'On peas? Certainly, brother.' Philip smiled and closed his eyes once more. Yes, he would think about those things, but for now he'd rather stay in this place of peace.

Philip sat like that for some time until another thought entered his head. He was curious about the monk sat dozing beside him. He opened his eyes to look at him. Hywel smelled ever so slightly of horses, and had removed his sandals, which were covered with muck, although his feet weren't much cleaner. Philip wanted to know more about this man who obviously loved being with his horses, and yet had sacrificed his time and energy to nurse a wounded soldier like him back to health.

'How did you come to be here? Hywel is a Welsh name, isn't it?' Philip asked tentatively.

'Here? Abbaye Grand Selve? You are right, this is not my home. I came here for three good reasons, and I have chosen to stay for one.'

'Oh?' Philip had hoped for a bit more. The monk, glancing at him, sighed heavily but continued.

'Hywel was not my birth name, but as my mother was Welsh-born and I had a deep affinity for Wales, I chose a Welsh name as my new name when I took orders. It means "eminent". That was a reflection of how I thought of myself at the time.' Hywel looked rueful at that. 'I actually live and work in a small community in Gwynedd, a quiet abbey by the banks of a flowing river, surrounded by forests and mountains.'

'Sounds idyllic.'

'It is. But it is also very cold in the winter and very wet most of the year!'

Still sounded good to Philip. Fresh air, wide-open spaces, plenty of trees and mountains to hide among.

'So you care for the horses there also?' he asked.

'Yes, I am horse master, an honorary term given to me by Prince Llewellyn himself. I breed and raise horses for him and his household. He pays the Abbey well, and the work suits me.'

'So why did you come here?' It was a bit like getting blood out of a stone, but Philip dared to push for more information.

'The first reason was to carry some important communications from the Cistercian abbeys in Wales to those in France. The letters I brought here will have been carried on to Clairvaux and Citeaux by another hand. The second reason was to seek out and purchase some horses of a specific breed, bred north of here. I want to improve the breeding stock at Abbey Cymer. The Welsh favour their small hill ponies but the prince wants horses that are bigger and stronger, but still light on their feet. Angevin horses are light and fast, so I thought to mate them with a larger horse, a destrier maybe, for the strength and size. I was going to look for such a stallion, until I met your Noble. Now, he is a fine piece of horseflesh. Not sure I'll be able to top him. I have the two mares I wanted, though, and who knows what might happen if I leave them alone with your horse?'

'You've already tried it, haven't you?' Philip glanced at him, grinning.

'Well, I might have just put them in a paddock together and forgotten about them for a few hours,' Hywel laughed.

'You said there was a third reason you came here to Grand Selve?'

'Yes. That would be Abbot Jerome. Or should I say *uncle* Abbot Jerome.'

'Ah! Family connections?'

'Yes. It isn't general knowledge, though, and I'd like it to stay that way.' Hywel gave Philip a quick, questioning look, and

Philip nodded in reply. 'Having an uncle as abbot here has been most helpful, to you and me both. Jerome was my father's younger brother, and whenever I am in France I make a point of coming here to see him. I don't expect favours from him, and am definitely not looking for advancement, although there might have been a time when I would have welcomed his aid in that. My uncle is getting on in years now, and I feel happier every time I have been able to see him in the flesh, and pray with him.'

Philip thought for a bit; it all made sense, but there was one other thing Hywel had said that he wanted to clarify. 'You stayed here for me, didn't you? I was the "one" reason you stayed.'

'Yes,' Hywel smiled. 'I was supposed to stay only a few days here, but it was on my way to Grand Selve that I came across you. I could have left you here in the care of Clement, but something urged me not to. I suppose you could say that I heard God speaking to me. He wanted me to stay, and the longer I stayed the less I wanted to leave, until I had seen you recover. I spoke with the abbot, and he agreed to let me stay as long as I worked for the Abbey while I was here, when I wasn't tending to your needs. They have a farm and vineyards, and cattle, sheep and goats. It is a much larger community than Cymer, but they need everyone living here to do their part to keep things running.'

'Now you are making me feel guilty. I could be doing more to help. I am almost recovered,' Philip said, shifting his position to emphasise the point.

'Physically, yes, you are. Thanks be to God!'

'So your obligation to me is almost ended, surely, and you will be returning to Wales soon?'

'I believe I must begin to plan for that, yes.' Hywel went back to contemplating the peas he still held in his hands.

Philip felt a twinge of sadness at the thought of being separated from this monk who had been his caregiver and had become his confidant, his companion – his friend. The realisation struck him. He hadn't had a real friend that he had trusted for a very long time, except that old horse of his. How strange that he would find such an unlikely friend here within abbey walls, of all places. What would become of him when Hywel left? He had no idea, and that panicked him. Hywel had talked about him burying his old life, but he could not imagine any other kind of life than the one he had become used to living before. He would have no idea where to go, or what to do next. Hopelessness threatened to overwhelm him.

Hywel must have sensed his unease and turned to look at him full in the face.

'Philip,' he said, 'I have a proposition for you.' His usually smiling face was still deeply serious. 'Come back to Wales with me.'

Philip was deeply moved and grateful for Hywel's offer, and he allowed himself a small smile of thanks. Inside he was struggling with his emotions. 'It is impossible.' He shrugged, sadly. 'I would not be welcomed back in Wales. Whatever life I choose to live now, I must accept that it must be away from the place I once loved the most.'

Hywel kept looking at him, obviously not satisfied with his answer. 'It may be difficult for you to return as Philip de Braose, I can see that. But what if you were to return as someone else?'

'A new identity? How? Disguise myself as an old begging woman? It would be the only way. I'm afraid too many people would know me as a man.' Philip laughed but it was pained.

'As a man maybe, but not as a monk.'

A monk? What was Hywel suggesting? He had said earlier that he didn't expect Philip to follow him into the Church. Had he changed his mind? Philip wasn't anywhere close to making that much of a drastic life change. Surely Hywel would know that.

Or *was* he ready? Perhaps he could do it. He'd tried everything else. The abbey life had lots to recommend it. But Philip knew that if he was going to take vows, he owed God more than a superficial desire for a quiet life. It wouldn't sit right with him to make false promises, and he wasn't sure he trusted

God fully enough yet to give Him the whole of the rest of his life.

Hywel was speaking again. 'Abbey Cymer is small and remote. We don't get many visitors, especially those of noble rank. Does Prince Llewellyn know you?'

'I met him once.' Philip ground his teeth at the memory. 'But it was a long time ago and I was a very different person then. Young – and naïve.'

'I think if we disguised you as a monk, for the journey, at least, we could get you through France and through Wales unrecognised.'

Oh, so a temporary disguise. That, perhaps, he could do. 'So I would come to Cymer with you?'

'For a while, yes. Until you are fully recovered.' Hywel was looking at him intently.

'Recovered? I thought I was almost there.' Philip subconsciously straightened out his left leg to demonstrate.

'I believe God has asked me to keep close to you until you are fully recovered. And not just physically. Your mind and heart and spirit have been wounded far more deeply than the wounds of your flesh. That inner recovery will take much longer, but I am confident that God wants to see you fully healed. He is the great redeemer and life restorer, I can testify to that in my own life. But as always, the choice is with you. You must decide what you must do.' Hywel swung around and held out his fist, opening it to drop the peas into Philip's lap. 'Just remember the peas.'

'I'm unlikely to forget!' Philip smiled at him.

'And now we must go.' Hywel heaved himself up off the bench and handed Philip his crutch, helping him to his feet and steadying him with his strong hand. 'I have talked too much and Brother Francis will be glad when we have done disturbing his solitude. God had a sense of humour, placing me with the Cistercians.' He smiled broadly back at Philip. 'We are supposed to be a silent order.'

Let me make this clear: A single grain of wheat will

never be more than

a single grain of wheat unless it drops into the

ground and dies.

Because then it sprouts and produces a great harvest

of wheat

– all because one grain died.

John 12:24, TPT

4
Easter

Over the following three weeks, Philip made good progress. Perhaps the thought of potentially leaving France was impetus enough. The walking was easier, and he was getting far less tired. He was spending time with Noble in the stables, and had managed to heave himself up onto the horse's back a couple of times. One particular afternoon he had got himself into the saddle, with not inconsiderable effort and the help of Noble's mane, and had handed the reins to Hywel. Noble seemed unusually happy just to be led around the courtyard with the weight of Philip on his back. The horse was patient and paced slowly, sensing that his rider was not completely comfortable. For Philip, this was no lack of confidence in his horsemanship, or a result of fear; rather, just the supreme physical effort it was taking to stay upright in the saddle.

'Won't be long before you are galloping him across fields again,' Hywel commented encouragingly, as he helped Philip in his ungainly dismount from the standing horse.

'Or riding across Welsh countryside, perhaps?' Philip answered.

'Yes, that too. Not long now.' Hywel said no more as he led Noble back towards the stable. Philip hobbled after him, stiff from his short ride.

Hywel secured Noble in his stall and turned when Philip approached. 'You have not been seen in the church yet, and it has been noticed. It has also been noticed that you are well enough to spend time with your horse.' It was not accusatory, just a statement of fact. So, Philip thought, he was being watched and maybe judged. He felt a tinge of guilt; it was hardly showing gratitude to the community of the Abbey, or to God, for that matter, for him to neglect attending church when he was clearly well enough to do so.

'Perhaps as this Sunday is Resurrection Sunday, it might be a good time for you to attend Mass? There will be a good number of people here and it will be a joyous occasion. You can hide in the crowd, but be seen at the same time, if you follow my meaning?' Hywel continued, while raking some fresh straw into Noble's stall. The monk was looking out for him, Philip realised.

'I can do that,' he replied. Inside, he was not so sure he could. It was a long time since he had ventured inside a church building – for the right reasons, anyway. He and God still had some things to settle. Unhelpful memories started to threaten and he felt his throat tighten. He helped Hywel settle the horse in silence before the two men walked back to the infirmary together. He probably didn't need to be here at the Abbey at all now, Philip thought to himself, taking up a bed and food that could be given to some other poor soul in need. It was time for him to leave. He only hoped the offer to leave with Hywel still stood.

Easter Sunday morning found him outside the church. The large, ornate wooden doors at the front of the Abbey church had been flung wide open to let the people of the local area into the tall building. The sun was shining bright and warm, and spring flowers were also celebrating the day, as vibrant pops of colour among the fresh green grass lining the path to the Abbey. The atmosphere was definitely celebratory, as groups of people came up the path chatting and laughing together, only falling silent, in a sort of imposed awe, as they stepped over the threshold of the door and into the quiet, cool church. Philip watched from a slight distance. Should he just follow in, attaching himself to a group of farmers? The simple dull tunic he was wearing would fit in; a loan from a lay brother, it felt rough against his skin. Not the fine quality he was used to wearing.

The monks used a separate entrance. They would file into the church via the side door directly leading from the cloister, within the Abbey enclosure, and sit themselves in the choir stalls closest to the high altar. Philip made a hasty decision. He turned and hurried back through the gate in the wall he had exited through, and around into the cloister. The bells were ringing a joyful chime, and the monks were silently making their way into the church. Philip held back until the last monk had entered and the bells had stopped ringing. He stepped to the side door that had been left ajar and inched his way silently around it, stepping from bright sunlight into the semi-dark interior of the church. He quietly made his way along the long side stone wall, trying not to be noticed, looking for a spot that he could occupy surreptitiously.

The singing of the chants had begun. It was a beautiful sound. Philip glanced back, taking in the great high windows that allowed light to stream in over the high altar, the high white columns and arches with their simple red and gold decoration, and the richly ornate gold cross that stood as a centrepiece on the altar. Then he looked over to the choir stalls and to the monks in their plain white habits, standing together, singing in unison. It should have felt wonderful, but in that moment something closer to terror engulfed Philip and he leaned hard against the stone wall, his body trembling. He had to get out. He made no sound that he was aware of, but he was screaming inside. Stumbling slightly, he made his way as quickly as he could back the way he had come and out of the church and into the cloister, breathing in the fresh air gratefully. He was free, but not free enough. He ran awkwardly through the cloister and towards the infirmary building, not stopping until he had run through the corridor and out into the herb garden beyond. He collapsed exhausted onto his bench and dropped his head into his hands. His heart was thumping and his breath came in rapid gasps.

Philip recognised that he needed to calm himself and willed his breathing to slow down, raising his head and leaning it back against the warm stone wall behind him, his eyes closed. He tried to focus on the sounds and scents of the garden, continuing to breathe deeply, until his heart rate slowed and he felt his taut body begin to relax slightly.

Something had triggered a memory, a terrifying one. The incense! That was it. The sight and sounds within the Abbey church had been wonderful, but the smell. The smell took him back to another place and another time. A memory he had tried very hard to bury.

He didn't know how long he sat there. Peace was hard to keep hold of. His mind kept trying to take him back in time. He willed himself to dwell in the present; to concentrate on the warm sunshine and how it felt on his skin, the sound of the birds singing, and the smell of the freshly green thyme disturbed by his feet. He was suddenly aware of a familiar bulk sitting down beside him. Hywel didn't speak; his presence was comfort enough. They sat together in silence for some time.

'Sorry,' Philip managed eventually. He stirred himself, and opened his eyes to acknowledge Hywel.

'I saw you enter, and I saw you leave,' Hywel replied. 'Do not apologise to me. God knows you must have had your reasons for leaving so abruptly.'

'The incense. I think it was the incense. The smell...' Philip shuddered slightly.

'Yes, I've heard it said that smells can evoke memories as powerfully as sights or sounds.'

They sat in silence while Philip tried to manage his swirling thoughts. What should he say? Was it wise to drag up the memories and expose them, or to keep them well buried? Except that it was obvious to him now that they weren't as well buried as he had hoped they were.

'It may help you to speak of it.' The words were soft from Hywel's mouth.

How did the man know what he was thinking so much of the time? So, should he tell him? Philip steeled himself to remember it all. It felt somehow safe to recall the horror of it with this genuinely godly man sitting close to him, within the solid walls of the Abbey garden. He leaned forward, his elbows on his knees.

'When I left my home in Wales,' he began, 'I came to France. I was running away from heartbreak, and in my youthful exuberance I thought the best thing I could do was to bury my feelings by immersing myself into a good cause. A seemingly godly cause. I had a faith in God then.' He paused to look at Hywel, who nodded for him to continue. 'I found myself in the Royal Court and as a de Braose I was welcomed, with a degree of suspicion, to be fair, but welcomed nevertheless. I bore the family name with its reputation, but I still felt I had to prove myself. When I heard about the Albigensian Crusade[2] and its fight against heresy I chose to align myself with that. I ended up fighting for the cause, eventually under the command of Humbert de Beaujeu, against Raymond of Toulouse. I was at the siege of Labecede and at Vareilles.' He paused again, remembering.

'It seemed like the crusade was accomplishing what it set out to do, but I was so naïve and so misled. I was mixing with the highest levels of nobility, and in my own mind I was fighting a real enemy for a noble cause. I killed men, but only ever in fair combat. We had the Pope and the whole of Mother Church behind us. It felt good. I knew there were some who took to burning crops and killing livestock, but I could distance myself from them. The cause was what mattered to me.

'And so I blinded myself to the atrocities that were happening all around me in the name of this so-called "noble"

---

[2] The crusade against the rise of Catharism (considered heretical by the Church) in Southern France.

crusade. Behind closed doors and, God forgive them, even within churches and holy buildings, men who called themselves "men of God" indulged in what I can only describe as pure evil. Men, women and children were interrogated, tortured, ravaged, flayed alive, killed. All in the name of purifying the Church.' Philip spat it out. He paused, breathing deeply, needing to calm himself. Hywel had said nothing. He was sitting with his eyes closed and his hands clasped together in his lap. His face gave nothing away. Yet Philip knew he was listening, likely praying too. He too closed his own eyes and went back to that dark place.

'I did not believe it until I saw it with my own eyes. In a small town not far south of here, I was staying in an inn for the night with some comrades, when I became aware of a commotion outside. I was told not to concern myself, that the local bishop had arrived with some men to sort out an issue with a recently exposed group of heretics. I was intrigued, however, and let myself quietly out of the inn, into the dark street, and followed the group at a distance. They had stopped outside a dwelling, a shop of some kind, I think, and the door was being battered down. I stood half-hidden behind a tree, and watched as they dragged a man out by his tunic. So far I was unconcerned, but then two more of the men went into the building and came out with the women. One, an older lady, was being dragged, screaming, by her hair; the other, a young girl – I would say no more than twelve – was being carried like a side of meat over the other brute's shoulder.

'A small stone church stood on a small rise above the town and it was to this church the three were taken. I saw no one else that night. It was as if the whole of the rest of the town had closed their shutters, eyes and ears to what was happening. I felt compelled to follow. It didn't feel right, but if this was truly God's work, why should I want to impede it in any way? I found myself in that church, half-hidden in the darkness behind a column. I saw and heard horrific things that night that I have tried to bury the memories of. Without much success, it seems.

There was a faint smell of incense lingering in that church, the same as you use here…' Philip shuddered again, and felt Hywel shift slightly beside him, becoming aware of the monk's warm hand resting lightly on his arm. He took another deep breath. It needed to be told, an exorcism of sorts.

'They tried to make the man recant. Well, they said that was what they were trying to do – but to me, it looked like they were succumbing to every evil desire within themselves. I watched at first, horrified, as they began to torture the man by every conceivable means, and then I looked to get out of there. But the door of the church was shut and there was no way I could leave without drawing attention to myself. I wanted to intervene, but there were five of them, including the bishop. I knew I stood no chance, and I slipped down behind that column, frozen in terror. I tried to block out the sounds of the screaming with my hands over my ears. They turned to the women when they had finished with the man, violating and abusing them terribly – that poor young girl!' He swallowed back the bile that rose to his throat.

He felt Hywel's hand tighten slightly on his arm.

'When they were finished with them, all three were dragged outside and hung from a tree in the churchyard. To this day I torture myself that I didn't do something, anything, to try to stop it. The bishop, the so-called "man of God", he didn't just condone what his men did, he fully participated in *all* of it – a look of evil pleasure on his face. At that moment something within me broke. If this was the Church, if this was God's work, if this was a holy man whom I was supposed to revere and look up to for my faith, then I wanted no part of it. God was lost to me.

'I left the command of Humbert, abandoned the cause, and attached myself to a band of mercenaries, a soldier for hire. With them I could fight and let out my rage, and kill and maim without conscience. I had seen, and was to see, many horrific things on battlefields, but nothing that haunted my dreams as much as what I had seen in that church that night. It was better to fight for money than for a false good cause, and it got me closer to my ultimate aim – to escape this life completely.'

There. He had said it. He sagged back against the wall, spent.

Hywel spoke then, softly. 'You have done well to speak it out. What was hidden in darkness has now been exposed to the light. And the light will overcome the darkness.'

Philip wasn't sure of his meaning, but his tone wasn't accusatory.

'You don't condemn me?' Philip felt the weight of his guilt and shame sitting heavily on him.

'I do not judge any man,' Hywel replied simply. 'God is more than capable of doing that, and much more fairly than I ever could.'

'Then God will surely judge me. What hope do I have, if that is the case?' Philip put his head in his hands.

He felt Hywel shift again, to face him, he presumed. His hand was still resting on Philip's arm. At least he hadn't pulled away in revulsion.

'God sees all. God knows you, Philip. He knows your heart. What you experienced has affected you so deeply, has caused you to grieve and feel shame and regret. That is the first step. God can forgive all who can repent.'

'Even those men who acted so abominably in God's name?' Philip looked up into Hywel's face, his own anger barely supressed. He was sure those foul men would never be deserving of God's mercy.

'You can be confident that God will judge them too, my son.' Hywel looked intently at him, deadly serious. 'They will be called to account, most especially for what they did, be in no doubt. Leave them to God. It is time for you to let go of any part you believe you played in their guilt.'

'By doing nothing it was as if I condoned it.'

'You were not responsible for their actions. Only they were.'

'Do you believe that I can really be free of this darkness inside me?' Philip sighed. The feelings of despair were not far from the surface again. 'I have witnessed much suffering, death and cruelty, and I have been the cause of some of it. I have suffered betrayal, and I have betrayed my own beliefs. I have taken out my frustrations on the undeserving, God included. I have done much that I am ashamed of.'

'As have we all.'

Philip doubted very much that Hywel had, but as he glanced up, he saw a flicker of pain cross the monk's face.

'I can assure you,' Hywel continued, 'sitting here with you, that as surely as the sun there will set and rise again tomorrow, there is hope that you can walk free from all of it. From darkness, into life-giving light. That is the message of Easter, is it not?' He held Philip's gaze. 'The followers of Jesus watched in horror as He was interrogated, tortured and hung on a cross to die, all by those who were supposedly acting in the name of God. As He hung there on that tree He uttered those extraordinary words: "Father, forgive them, for they do not know what they do."[3] It is supposed that He was referring to the soldiers tasked with His execution, but what if that forgiveness was being extended to all who had played a part in His death? To those who had orchestrated and ordered it, those who stood mocking Him as He died, even to His followers who had denied and abandoned Him?'

Hywel paused briefly to let his words settle, watching Philip's face all the time. He continued, 'And then, after three days buried in a tomb, the women came to grieve Him and found He had risen. Jesus had passed from death to life, defeating darkness and rising into glorious light. And so, yes, I believe each of us can be free of the power of darkness, because of the resurrection. God offers forgiveness and light to us all.' Hywel ended there.

Philip was vaguely aware of a bell ringing, a call to prayer, no doubt, but in that moment it felt more like a celebratory peel. He needed time to think and process.

'I must go,' Hywel rose to his feet.

---

[3] Luke 23:34, NKJV.

'I will come with you.'

'To the church? You are ready?' Hywel looked back questioningly.

Philip shrugged. 'I think I need to be.'

Hywel smiled then and turned, tucking his hands into his sleeves in front of him, adopting the serene aspect expected of a Cistercian attending the offices. He began to walk, slightly more hurriedly than he was perhaps supposed to, towards the cloister and church beyond. Philip stood gingerly to his feet and followed after him. This time as he entered the church, Philip focused his attention on the cross displayed on the altar. As he sat down he let the music the monks sang wash over him, and he began to do what he had not done for a very long time. He began to pray.

But if we freely admit our sins when his light

uncovers them,

he will be faithful to forgive us every time. God is just

to forgive us our sins

because of Christ,

and he will continue to cleanse us from all

unrighteousness.

1 John 1:9, TPT

5
The Prodigal

Once all the festivities surrounding Easter were done, Hywel and Philip planned to take their leave from Abbey Grand Selve as soon as it could be arranged. Hywel had been away from Cymer and his horses for far longer than he had intended, and it would take them many days to make the long journey back.

Philip felt he was ready for the ride, but Hywel seemingly had his doubts as to how fast and how far they would be able to travel each day. They had Noble, and Hywel's own horse, and they also had the two mares that he had purchased, so they would at least be able to alternate and rest the horses. They would also travel light. Hywel had very little and Philip had even less. He had enquired after his armour and weaponry but it would not be coming back with them. His hauberk had been gifted to the Abbey, and the other clothing he had been wearing when he had been found was in no fit state to be kept. Hywel had found no sword on Philip's person, assuming it had been dropped when he was injured, but his sword belt and a small dagger had been kept safe for him. These were presented to Philip as they loaded the horses with saddlebags containing a change of clothes, and a sack of provisions for the journey.

Philip took the items from Hywel's hand. They had been cleaned and carefully wrapped in sackcloth. The sword belt looked a bit worse for wear but the leather could be repaired, he supposed, if he should ever need its use again. The dagger he was pleased to see. It had been made for him in Swansea. A gift from his brother John. It bore the letters 'DB', for de Braose, engraved on its pommel, with a single red garnet embedded between them. The leather grip was intact and smooth, and the cross-guard still beautifully gilded. Philip held it in his hand and moved it around, remembering the weight and feel of it. The short blade and tip were still sharp, he discovered. He would carry the weapon on his person somehow. He felt he needed some sort of protection at hand. He was still not sure of their safety on the journey that awaited them. The sword belt, however, would have to be hidden among their possessions. It definitely would be incongruous worn with a Cistercian habit.

Philip rubbed his hand ruefully over his tonsured head. It definitely felt cooler without a full head of hair and it would be a great deal easier to look after. His own brown curls had become long and unruly during his convalescence. He preferred being clean shaven again too; Brother Clement had proven himself extremely proficient with a razor.

The previous evening Philip had stood before Abbot Jerome for him to approve the transformation from man to monk. He had also hoped to be able to thank him in person for permitting his stay at the Abbey, for the care he had received, and for being complicit in creating his new identity. He supposed it would be quite irregular within the Order for a lay person to pretend to be a monk, but Hywel's influence with his uncle had obviously prevailed and he had granted permission for Philip to be shaved and clothed as a full Cistercian brother. When they went to Abbot Jerome's private quarters to meet with him, they had found the abbot sitting in a chair pulled close to a lit fire, which made the small room feel stiflingly warm. He was wearing the same dull white habit as all of the brothers, but had around his shoulders a rich blue fine woollen cloak with a gold clasp. Philip could see that he had once been a tall man, but age had stooped his proud back. He had the same warm brown eyes as Hywel had, but his were dulled with age. His face was kind, however.

'Hywel tells me that you feel this disguise is necessary for your safety?' the abbot had enquired. His voice was not strong but held authority.

'Yes, my lord,' Philip had replied, bowing slightly from the waist.

'Call me Father Abbot, and I don't require your obeisance.' The older man had smiled then, and the family resemblance with Hywel was even more compelling. Philip had found himself staring. How was it possible that the two men kept their family connection secret? He had started when he realised that the abbot was speaking again.

'I will not keep you long, as I know you wish to leave at sunrise, but I do want to say this. We who wear this habit have all had to take sacred vows, consecrating ourselves to God and to the rules of the Order. It would not be right for you to take those vows at this stage, and yet I have let you assume your identity as one of us. I require, therefore, that you do nothing to make me regret that decision. Your conduct and your speech and your attitude must be in line with what I would expect of any monk of this order. Whatever your experience of holy men outside these walls,' he had glanced over to Hywel at that, 'I urge you to remember the care and acceptance that you have experienced here, and repay that by not doing anything to bring this house into disrepute. Hywel here will keep you in line, and teach you all that you need to know to pass yourself off as a Cistercian brother. Listen to him, but above all, watch him and follow his example. He is not perfect, but has a character well refined and tested by adversity, and he loves God truly. You could do no better than to learn from him.'

Abbot Jerome had then nodded to Hywel and held out a shaky hand. Hywel had stepped forward and taken the proffered hand and bent over as if to kiss it, but then he had leaned forward and kissed the old man on the cheek. Jerome had pushed him away playfully. 'Enough!' he laughed. 'I pray you both God speed, until we meet again. Here or in eternity.'

'I wanted to offer my thanks…' Philip had started to speak, wanting to try to voice the overwhelming gratitude that he felt, but the abbot had already closed his eyes, rested his head back against the chair, and indicated with his hand for them to leave.

Philip and Hywel had walked back together in silence, Philip even more aware of the enormity of wearing the habit, as he kept in step with his companion.

'You will thank him for me?' Philip had asked as they reached the infirmary door.

'I have already. I don't think I will speak to him again in this life.' Hywel was thoughtful, but not sad. 'He is deserving of his heavenly reward. He is a good man, and has been a great uncle to me.'

He had paused, before turning to Philip. 'Get some rest now. We leave at first light.'

The first day of their journey started well. Although the sky was overcast, the air was warm, and several sunny days had left the tracks and paths dry and well compacted, making it easy for the horses' hooves. Philip was enjoying being on horseback again and being free from the confines of the Abbey, taking in the trees and fields, and wide open sky. Noble seemed to be enjoying the ride also, trotting along with his great head nodding slightly, alert as usual, looking for the next adventure. Hywel was, as expected, an exceptional horseman, and he led the way confidently mounted on a fine bay, while also leading the two mares he had bought.

Philip had felt a tinge of sadness as they had left Grand Selve. Clement had come to the stables to wave them off, his kind face all smiles, and several of the brothers and lay brothers had gathered, including the elusive Brother Francis, to nod their farewells as Philip and Hywel had passed through the Abbey gates. That place and those brothers would hold a special place in his heart, but Philip was glad to be leaving, glad to have Hywel as his companion, glad to be returning to Wales. He was nervous as to what might lie ahead for him, but also excited. He had spoken to God and made a fragile agreement with Him. He would give this new life a chance. God would still have to prove Himself trustworthy, though. One thing he was sure of: he wanted to be a better man, and live a better life. He looked ahead at the man riding the horse in front of him. He wanted to be more like Hywel.

As the day wore on, the excitement and pleasure of the ride diminished. Philip's body was beginning to ache with the effort of staying in the saddle, and his knee was throbbing disconcertingly. Added to that, the overcast sky had started to drop occasional huge drops of rain, and the air had turned from warm to decidedly muggy.

'Not much liking the look of those skies,' Hywel said, pulling up so that Philip could come alongside. 'I had hoped that the weather would have held dry and that we could have found a sheltered spot among some trees to rest for the night. Now it looks like we will need to find a sheltered spot with an actual roof. I don't want you to get soaked and risk your fever returning.'

Philip looked around; he could see no recognisable landmarks, just more trees and fields in all directions. 'Do you know where we are?'

Hywel nodded. 'We have made decent progress, but we are not near enough to any reasonably sized settlement, by my estimation. I think we will just have to pray that God provides a farm, or smallholding, with a welcoming host, or even an abandoned building. As you can guess, not all of the people around here would necessarily welcome two Cistercian monks and four horses turning up seeking shelter.'

They rode on in silence for a few more miles. The rain started to fall more steadily and they pulled their hoods up to protect their heads. The odd rumble of thunder and distant flash of lightning made the horses skittish. It was also getting darker by the minute.

'There,' Philip called ahead to Hywel, who had his head down, trying to keep his face out of the now driving rain, 'a building. Ahead to your right.'

Galvanised by the faint light showing from the window of the rough wooden dwelling, they spurred their horses towards it. It was a long, low, humble house with a central door and a window to the right. At the far end was another, smaller, open doorway, the whole building covered by a simple thatch. As they approached, the main door opened and a bearded face appeared, holding a flickering candle.

'Brothers!' The voice was gruff and heavily accented. 'What brings you to our door?' There was a definite hint of suspicion.

'We are looking for nothing more than a roof over our heads for the night, if it is possible?' Hywel called back, in a pleasant tone.

The man stepped slightly out of the doorway, glancing behind him into the house. 'We have little enough room for ourselves here, and my wife and the little ones are tucked up for the night. You would not have me disturb them?'

'No, no, my friend, of course not!' Hywel had dismounted and was trying to soothe the three horses in his control. 'Is there an animal shed, a stable, anything? We would just be grateful for a roof of any kind tonight.'

The man paused for a moment and nodded. He had seemingly decided to trust them. 'I have no stable as such, but you can tie the horses up with mine over there.' He nodded to where a crooked-backed old nag was tied up under a canopy formed by two spreading oak trees. 'The grass is long and needs trimming over there, so they can graze to their hearts' content.'

Noble would not be that content, Philip smiled to himself, either with the accommodation or the company, having been quite spoiled with his dry stable at the Abbey. But the horse would have food enough, at least.

'You two are welcome to shelter in with the animals. I am afraid because of the weather I have brought the pig and the goat inside, but there is plenty of fresh straw in there for you to rest on, and at least you will be out of this storm.' A loud crack of thunder over their heads seemed to punctuate his words.

'That is a fine offer. We would be pleased to accept,' Hywel nodded and smiled as the water dripped from his hood.

We would? thought Philip. Could they not go on a few miles in the hope of finding an inn of some kind? But it seemed that Hywel had decided they were stopping here.

They led the horses over to the tree canopy, which was surprisingly dry under the branches, and tied the horses lightly. 'I hope they don't bolt,' Hywel sighed, as the two of them turned and made a dash back towards the farm building. The farmer was standing by the other open doorway. Hywel and Philip both ducked through the low opening and came face to face with an enormous pig, who grunted with displeasure at the new arrivals. The farmer appeared behind them.

'She is harmless, just a bit grumpy,' he said, indicating the sow. 'There is fresh enough water in the pail over there, I raised it from the well earlier,' he nodded to the corner, 'and the straw is clean. I cannot offer you food, but there will be fresh goat's milk in time for you to break your fast in the morning. My wife will see to that.' He nodded over to the back of the room where, in the shadows, Philip could just make out the shape of a small goat. It stood watching them, chewing nonchalantly.

'No, no, thank you,' Hywel was all reassurance. 'We have provisions here.' He indicated the sack in his hands. 'We will do well enough. Thank you again for your kind hospitality.'

As the farmer turned to leave, Philip thought that perhaps Hywel had gone over the top a bit with his thanks, especially when his nose registered just how smelly the pig was. Hardly luxurious accommodation, and their host wasn't the most congenial of fellows. Still, what was it that Hywel had taught him about being grateful... for the small things? They were out of the rain and it was warm, at least.

Hywel was already settling down on a pile of straw. The pig had snuffled away. Philip resigned himself to the situation and dropped down to sit by Hywel, who was retrieving a loaf of bread from the sack.

'Here, eat this,' he said, as he passed a chunk to Philip. 'There is ale left in the flagon to wash it down, too. Then I suggest we try to get as much sleep as we possibly can. I suspect our animal companions will be early risers.' He laughed softly to himself.

Philip ate his supper, and by the time he had finished it, Hywel was already curled on his side and snoring softly; the sleep of the peaceful. Philip doubted he would settle so quickly. The exhaustion of the ride, however, combined with a day of fresh air had him asleep not so long after Hywel.

He was shaken awake. It was pitch black but he could make out Hywel's face looming over him and feel the weight of his hand resting heavily on his shoulder.

'What? Is it morning yet?' It didn't make sense that it was, by the darkness of the room.

'Sorry to wake you, my friend, but you were calling out so loudly in your sleep that I thought you might wake our hosts on the other side of that wall. By the sweat on your brow and the way you are trembling, I would guess it was another bad dream.'

Philip closed his eyes and the half-memory of a dream flickered through and then was lost to him. 'If it was, I can't remember it. That's progress, I suppose.'

'I would say so. If your dreams are less frequent and less disturbing, that would indicate your mind is finding more peace.'

'What time would you say it is?' Philip was wide awake now.

'Vigils, or so my monk's body would tell me. I was already awake before you started shouting.'

The storm had stilled outside, and the inside of the dwelling was now steaming with the warmth of their bodies, the dampness of their clothes and the all-pervading stink of their animal companions.

'I have no light and wouldn't chance a candle in here anyway, but I can feel around for the flagon, if you need a drink.'

'I would appreciate that.' Philip's mouth was dry as dust.

He heard Hywel scuffling around and then he handed him the ale and they both took a swig. Philip rearranged the straw beneath him, but was guessing that sleep would not return easily.

'This place reminds me of a story.' Hywel had obviously picked up that Philip was still agitated, and not being one to miss an opportunity, he obviously had some middle-of-the-night wisdom to impart. Philip was glad to hear the soothing lull of his voice. I'll let him tell his story, he thought to himself. It might just put me to sleep before he's finished.

'Go on,' he whispered, lying back down.

'There was once a wealthy landowner. He had two sons. He was a loving and generous man and his two sons were brought up lacking nothing. However, they did lack character. Both were self-centred and lacked true respect and care for their father, or for his feelings. One day the younger son came to his father, who had never refused him anything, and asked for his inheritance early. As was the law of the land, all that the landowner possessed would be divided equally between his sons on his death. However, this boy could not wait for his father's death, and wanted what he felt was owed him.'

'You speak as if you know this family?' Philip could hear emotion in Hywel's voice.

Hywel paused, and breathed out a sigh, 'Not this one, but one very like it.'

'So what did the landowner do?'

'He gave the boy what he asked for.'

'That was asking for trouble!'

'Indeed. The immature young man took the vast amount of money that his father gave him and left home, breaking his father's heart. He travelled around, spending his inheritance on all the things that young men think they want. He got drunk, and got his friends drunk. He partied, he paid for women, he gambled, he made friends by buying them with his money, until one day he realised that every penny had gone. And with his money went all his so-called friends and associates. He was left alone and in abject poverty. Eventually he managed to beg work from a farmer, not unlike our host. The farmer took him on, but did not offer the boy any wages, but in exchange for looking after the pigs, he said he could sleep with them and eat the food they ate.'

Philip didn't have to imagine the awfulness of that, sitting there with the foul-smelling pig breathing right by his ear. He snorted in disgust. 'Some would say that he got what he deserved for treating his family so coldheartedly and for wasting his inheritance so foolishly.' He paused, as another thought came. 'But you have shown me to be careful how I judge others. Who can say how anyone else should or shouldn't behave? I've done enough that I'm ashamed of, that is much more deserving of punishment than this lad.'

'It isn't the end of the story, though,' Hywel continued. 'For the whole time that his son had been away, the father had looked out for him. Every day he would go out and search for him, or stand at the threshold of his property just looking out, watching and hoping for his wayward son to return. He still loved him, and was deeply concerned for him. He desperately wanted him home, despite what he had done.

Sitting in his pigsty one day, the boy looked around at his surroundings and realised something – that even the servants in his father's household lived better than he was living. He was desperately ashamed of what he had done, and wondered if there was any way he could return to his family, even if he could perhaps become a servant. He decided he would return home, and beg his father's forgiveness, and take his chances. He got himself up out of his self-made pit and headed home.

'Before he had got anywhere near his old home, he saw a figure come running towards him. Terrified, he thought his father had sent out a guard to beat him off. He fell to his knees, sobbing in desperation. But then he realised it was no guard, but his father himself. And he carried no weapon, but instead his face was wreathed with joy. The father ran to his son, grabbed him, stood him to his feet, and then gathered him into his arms and wept on his neck.'

Hywel paused, and the emotion was palpable in the air between them.

'That's an extraordinary act of mercy on the part of the father.' Philip wanted to hear more – if the reconciliation was real and lasting. How it worked out for them. It touched something in his own soul. A longing; for what, he was not sure.

'Mercy, yes, and unconditional love. It went even further than his father welcoming him with outstretched arms. The father wouldn't hear of his son becoming a servant. He restored him straight away to his place of honour within the family, clothed him with the finest clothes, put the family ring back on his finger, gave him the best sandals money could buy, and then threw a huge welcome home party, inviting all his friends and neighbours to celebrate with them.'

'You said there was another brother? Where was he in all of this?'

'He had stayed with his father, but was proud and arrogant and self-righteous. He was angry when his brother returned, and particularly that he got so much attention from his father. He couldn't see how he deserved it. He insulted his father by not attending the celebrations, and made his feelings obvious to anyone who would listen. In his own way he showed as much disregard for his father's feelings as his brother had. And a lack of gratitude for what he had always had made him both bitter and entitled. His father had to remind him of all that he had been given, all the blessings that were his, just because he was his son. All he wanted was for both of his sons to understand that truth. That whether they left or whether they stayed, they would always be his sons, and he would always love them.'

'How did they work it all out?' Philip desperately wanted there to be a happy ending, but he was painfully aware that real-life relationships don't always end happily.

'That I don't know,' Hywel said softly.

'Oh. So that is the end of your story?' Philip was disappointed.

'It's where Jesus ended it. But His story illustrated an extraordinary truth which many of His listeners would have understood. The landowner in the story is God, our heavenly Father, and the sons represent us – human beings. We can all know God's love and blessing, but some of us choose to take what He has given us and squander it, while others live with ingratitude and a feeling of entitlement and self-righteousness. All He wants is for us to come back to Him with repentant hearts and He will embrace us and celebrate us, and restore us to right relationship with Him. Living as God's son in a close, love relationship with Him is the absolute best. It is what we were designed for.'

'But that father in the story didn't even care what the son had done. He didn't judge him for it or hold it over him. That boy didn't get the punishment he deserved, and instead got the honour he didn't deserve. God surely can't turn a blind eye to our sin?'

'That is the point, Philip. There is nothing, absolutely nothing, that you or I, or anyone, has done that will stop God from loving us and welcoming us back to Him with open arms. We need to repent, to admit our wrong, but He couldn't stop loving us and wanting us, not for anything. He is calling all His sons back home.'

'You said before that I needed a new identity. You weren't just talking about this guise, were you?' Philip pulled at his habit, thoughtfully.

'No. You need a different kind of new identity, but it is one that God has always offered you. The right to be called His son.'

Philip thought for a long moment. 'And He will accept me despite my filthiness?' It was a whisper.

'Without doubt, Philip. He is standing waiting with his arms outstretched right now, looking out for your return.'

It went quiet between them then.

'Good story,' Philip said, eventually.

'The best.' Philip heard Hywel settle back down onto his straw bed. The monk was almost instantly snoring again.

It was not the same for Philip. It was a long few hours until dawn, but it was in those quiet night hours where he did real business with God. He ran home, and God met him. Right there in that steaming, stinking pig shed.

From a long distance away, his father saw him

coming, dressed as a beggar,

and great compassion swelled up in his heart for his

son who was returning home.

So the father raced out to meet him. He swept him up

in his arms, hugged him dearly,

and kissed him over and over with tender love.

Then the son said, 'Father, I was wrong. I have

sinned against you. I could never deserve

to be called your son. Just let me be –'

The father interrupted and said, 'Son, you're home

now!'

Turning to his servants, the father said, 'Quick,

bring me the best robe,

my very own robe, and I will place it on his

shoulders. Bring the ring, the seal of sonship,

and I will put it on his finger. And bring out the best

shoes you can find for my son.

Let's prepare a great feast and celebrate. For this

beloved son of mine was once dead,

but now he's alive again. Once he was lost, but now

he is found!'

And everyone celebrated with overflowing joy.

Luke 15:20-24, TPT

6

Worship

Philip must have slept at some point, and it had been a deep, dreamless, restful sleep. When he awoke, the sun was streaming in through the open doorway, every vestige of the previous night's storm had gone, and the sky outside was a clear, bright blue. He woke up feeling lighter and more rested than he had for a very long time. He also woke up alone. The animals had gone from the shed and so had Hywel. Philip stretched out his stiff limbs. His habit felt damp, and he needed a drink and – his stomach grumbled – food. He hadn't quite mastered the ability the Cistercians seemed to have to fast for long periods of the day. Most of the monks ate only one meal a day at midday, exceptions being made for the youngest, eldest and the infirm, who might be permitted a simple breakfast and supper. He wondered if Hywel had eaten breakfast today, whether he would relax the rule on their journey.

Blinking, he emerged out of the dark shed and into the bright sunlight of the farmer's yard, which was more muddy puddles than anything else. He looked around. A small, round woman was feeding a group of scrawny-looking chickens. There were several children of various sizes doing various things around the yard, most of them involving mud. There was no sign of Hywel, but thankfully all four of their horses were standing nonchalantly grazing under the trees where they had been left. The farmer's horse was also missing.

'Good morning to you.' The farmer's wife had a surprisingly imposing voice for a little person. She had put down the chicken feed and was walking towards him with a plate and cup in her hands.

'Here, brother, break your fast.' She nodded to a stool leaning against the house wall.

'Thank you for your trouble.' Philip replied, taking the plate and cup from her, and sitting himself down clumsily on the low stool. It was a fair way down for his long legs. Made for her, obviously.

'Oh, it was not as much trouble as you think. Your friend had milked the goat for us before I even got up this morning.' She was smiling sweetly, her round face framed by straggly fair hair poking out from under a simple cap. 'I mixed up the oat cakes but he offered to stand over the fire and cook them, which is also something I am grateful for, with so many little ones to see to. It was a real blessing.'

Hywel. He was ever-surprising. No end to his talents, it seemed. Philip smiled back at her. 'Sorry I could not be as much help.'

'Oh, you will be,' she chuckled. 'They are waiting for you over there, as soon as you have eaten.' She indicated a group of trees at the far side of a field adjoining the farmhouse. 'The storm brought a tree branch down and my husband wants to retrieve the wood and bring it back here to use for firewood. The other brother offered your help.' She laughed at the look of consternation on Philip's face.

Philip managed a small smile in return. So they weren't leaving to continue their journey just yet, then? He enjoyed the fresh flat oat cakes and the warm goat's milk, and then made his way over to where he could see Hywel and the farmer tying a rope around a huge tree branch. The other end of the rope was tied to a harness on the farmer's horse.

'Nice of you to join us,' Hywel said teasingly, as Philip approached. 'Trust you slept well, brother?'

The farmer said nothing, just glanced up, grunted and nodded, before continuing with what he was doing. Working together, they got the tree branch back to the dwelling, half-leading, half-pushing the horse, and heaving the lump of wood between them. The horse was surprisingly strong, but it had needed all of them to manhandle the branch across the uneven, muddy field. All four of them, horse included, were puffing and blowing by the time they had the branch back. The farmer handed around a pail of freshly drawn well water with a ladle, and they all drank deeply.

'I can take my time in cutting that up now. My thanks for your help, brothers,' the farmer nodded as he sauntered away.

'I think that is us dismissed!' Philip said.

'It is time we were on our way anyway,' Hywel replied, wiping his grubby hands on his once-white habit, and heading over to where the horses stood waiting for them.

Before long they had mounted and taken their leave from the smallholding, waving their goodbyes to the row of muddy-faced children who had clambered onto the fence to see them off. They rode side by side in companiable silence, relaxed in the saddle, leading a mare each. The day was beautiful after the previous night's storm. Warm and dry, without being too hot. It was very pleasant indeed to be out in open countryside on horseback.

'So I can call you "brother" truly now?' Hywel's words came out of nowhere and caught a day-dreaming Philip by surprise. He smiled to himself. Hywel was not a prying person, but it was obvious he wanted to know what had happened to Philip during the night. Perhaps he had picked up on the quiet joy and peace that Philip seemed to be exuding. He knew what Hywel was asking, but wasn't going to make it easy for him.

'Well, I am supposed to be a brother in this guise, aren't I? Which reminds me… We need to think of a name for me to go by. I can't risk Brother Philip.' He smiled. 'And yes, brother, I have returned to my heavenly Father, and I believe He has accepted me – as His son.'

It had been said lightly but it was huge, and it brought a lump to his throat. He knew with every fibre of his being that he had a new identity now that would change his life forever. And if God could love him that much, forgive him for so much, then Philip thought that perhaps he was ready to trust Him with his whole life. He continued, 'I don't understand it all yet, but I know something happened inside me last night.'

'I guessed as much. God certainly had His reasons for our unusual overnight accommodation, it seems,' Hywel laughed. 'And don't worry about what you don't yet understand. You will spend the rest of your life learning what life as God's child looks like. I'm still learning, every day.'

They rode on together in silence for a while longer. Philip felt a growing excitement within him that hadn't been there before, and hope – yes, hope – that was not just of his own choosing. A knowing, a deep knowing that his life could now have meaning and purpose. He wanted to just sit in that feeling for a while.

'Robert.' Hywel broke the silence again.

'Sorry?' Philip was lost.

'Brother Robert, that's what we'll call you. It was my father's and my brother's name, so I'm not likely to forget it. It means "bright glory", or something like that.'

'Oh. A lot to live up to, then!'

'I think it suits you; how you look today, anyway. Your face is glowing.'

'You know what "Philip" means, don't you?' Philip said. 'It means "horse lover"!'

Hywel laughed out loud. 'Well, that fits too because that is the role you are going to play from now on. If asked, I will explain that you are a keen horse lover who has agreed to come back to Wales with me to help me in my breeding programme.'

'Well, that is not so far from the truth. I think I can fit that role well enough,' Philip laughed with him, reaching down to pat Noble's neck. 'What do you think, Noble?' The horse snorted in what sounded suspiciously like derision.

The journey from Abbaye Grand Selve to the bustling port of Bordeaux took them many days. Hywel had estimated maybe five days and it had taken nearer seven. Partly because Philip was not as physically strong as he wanted to be and couldn't stay in the saddle for long periods of time without experiencing pain in his leg and back, and partly because Hywel kept slowing them down, stopping for the oddest of reasons.

Hywel had surprised Philip at the farm on that first night, and he continued to surprise him along the whole journey. He would stop just to speak to people, or sometimes to offer his help to someone in need. There had been the cart stuck in the ditch that Hywel, and a reluctant Philip, had helped to pull free. Then there was the wizened old woman whom Hywel had dismounted for. She was standing up to her wrinkled knees in a stream, picking watercress. Hywel had taken off his sandals, hoisted up his habit and stepped into that stream before Philip had even properly halted his horses. He had watched as the large monk had gently taken the basket from the woman's arm, and helped her out of the stream, before plunging back in and picking a mound of watercress for her.

In one village they had stopped for provisions at a baker's shop. Hywel had paused to talk to a woman as he came out of the shop and then disappeared with her, returning in a few moments empty-handed. Smiling over at Philip, he had dipped back into the shop and bought more bread, which actually made it into their saddlebags.

They had slept under the stars when they could, but one night they had stopped for the night at a small hostelry. It wasn't overly clean, but the food had been edible and the ale superb. After a couple of nights sleeping outside, it had been nice to sleep in a bed for a night, and to have clean well water to wash their faces. Philip had thought that they would retire early, that an inn's parlour was not the place for two Cistercian monks to loiter in, but Hywel surprised him again. He had joined a group of working men at a table, and sat drinking with them, talking and laughing. Philip had sat quietly watching at a distance, nursing his ale and wondering who exactly this friend of his was.

Eventually they arrived late one afternoon at the outskirts of Bordeaux. Hywel stopped his horse by a cluster of huge rocks on a headland that overlooked the sea. Below them they could see the ships in the harbour, and sailors and traders bustling about. It was a large town, with many impressive stone buildings, grown prosperous from its trade in local wine.

'We'll rest here for a few hours,' Hywel said. 'I need to go into town at first light to see if we can get passage on a cargo ship sailing to England. They sail to Bristol from here and that would suit us well.'

'It would mean just a short trip from Bristol across the river estuary and into Wales?'

'Yes, not such a short trip to get there from here, though.' Hywel shuddered slightly.

Interesting, Philip thought. Not a keen sailor, then?

They made their camp and lit a small fire to warm them and the last of their ale. There was only a crust of bread left in their provisions sack, and Hywel insisted Philip had it. They watched the sun going down together, their backs against a rock and their legs outstretched in front of them.

'Can I ask you something?'

Hywel had closed his eyes, but Philip didn't think he was asleep.

'Ask away,' Hywel replied, not opening his eyes.

'I thought that monks were supposed to live their lives in seclusion, in enclosed communities away from the outside world, cut off from ordinary people. But you seem to take every opportunity to be with people. Even if it means inconveniencing yourself, us, our plans.'

Hywel snorted. 'Was that a veiled complaint, brother?' He sat up and looked intently at Philip. 'We live in a community, yes, and a silent one at that, which I admit isn't always easy for me. But we aren't completely cut off from the outside world. We serve our local people also. We take remedies to the sick, we pray with the dying, and we provide for those who are hungry or lacking clothes. I work beside the humblest of men who come to help us harvest our crops, and deal with princes and nobles who come to buy our horses. But I admit I do like the opportunities to interact a bit more naturally with people that being on the road affords me.'

'You stopped for people that others would have passed by, as you did for me when I was wallowing half-dead in that roadside ditch,' Philip continued. 'Staying to help the farmer and his wife when we were already late in starting out on our second day, I questioned that. You seemed to go above and beyond; you even milked the goat, for goodness' sake!' Philip's tone was teasing but the questioning serious. 'I know you wanted to show your thanks for their hospitality, but it felt like it meant something more to you than that?'

Hywel didn't reply straight away.

'What do you think worship is, Philip?' That was an unexpected question, but Philip was getting used to Hywel now, and knew he hadn't forgotten what he had asked him. He went with it.

'Well, I have heard the beautiful sound of your brother monks singing their psalms and songs. It must rise to heaven in worship. It certainly stirred my soul and I am sure it blessed God.'

'Indeed, if it is from the heart, then singing God's praise is worship. But true worship isn't just about singing. Which is just as well in my case.'

'I have never heard you sing, Hywel.' Philip wasn't going to let that comment go. Had he discovered a flaw in this seemingly flawless man?

'And you don't want to.' Hywel grimaced. 'Not all Welsh men can sing, believe me. Although I can sing as well as anyone in my heart. True worship is about our heart response to God. It should come out of a deep love for Him, and appreciation for all He has done for us. The form that worship takes is not restricted to singing or church services. It can be expressed in many different ways. Some people worship by painting beautiful pictures, or growing stunning flower gardens, for example. When I stopped to help that farmer's family after the storm it was because love compelled me. Love and thankfulness to God, for providing for us, in answer to our need. It gave me an opportunity to express God's love and our thankfulness to our humble hosts. I saw it as an act of service, but also as an act of worship to God.'

'I see… I think.' Actually, Philip thought that this might be another of those things he might need some time to understand fully. 'And the others that you stopped for?' he asked.

'As we rode, I talked to God. I find being on horseback, surrounded by the beauty of creation, is one of the best places I know to pray without distraction. I would ask God as we passed through villages and settlements to point out to me people He wanted me to stop for or to speak to,' Hywel continued. 'The widow in the stream, she hadn't spoken to another soul for many days. She was grateful for the watercress which she could sell for a few pennies, but she was even more grateful for a few kind words and a smile from a fellow human being.

'The woman outside the bakery? She was beside herself with worry, as her children had not eaten for two days. I went home with her and she fed her children with our provisions, but it was my prayers for her children's health and prosperity that moved her to tears.

'The men in the tavern? They were reminiscing about a friend of theirs who had died exactly a year to the day in a sad accident. They were laughing at their memories of him, while deeply grieving too. I felt by just being with them I could release some of the comfort of God to their souls. They spoke openly in front of me of their fears about their future and for their families, seeing how their friend's death had left his family destitute. I could not give them answers but I was a listening ear, and they seemed to appreciate that.'

Hywel stopped then. He wasn't looking for Philip's approval, he was just answering honestly. Philip accepted his reticence to say more. He knew enough about the inherent humility of the man already.

'So explain to me again what the connection is to worship?'

Hywel had leaned back and closed his eyes again, but he opened them to look over at Philip as he answered him. 'God gave everything He had for our salvation. He gave his only Son. Then, when we return to Him as Father, He loads us with even more good things: peace, joy, hope and many more blessings besides, as you are just beginning to experience. What then is our rightful response to all He has given us? What could we possibly give back to Him?'

'I have nothing apart from my horse and a few meagre belongings now. What could I possibly give to God?' And then he knew the answer. 'I have nothing to give Him but myself,' Philip whispered. It was the realisation of a powerful truth.

'Which is all any of us have to give Him,' Hywel replied softly, 'and all that He ever asks of us.'

'So worship is giving of ourselves back to God, expressed in how we live our lives?' It was beginning to make sense. It was stirring inside Philip, that desire to give his whole life as a thank offering back to God. To somehow express how grateful he was… for everything.

'Exactly that. Every time we help someone else in Christ's name, especially when it inconveniences us, it is an act of worship. Every time we give our time, strength and minds to doing the things that God wants us to do, rather than doing what we would prefer to do, that is our sacrifice of praise to Him.'

Philip looked at the gentle giant of a man sitting relaxed next to him. He knew that he was a long way from being the self-sacrificial man that Hywel was, but his friend was inspiring him at every step to be the better man that he knew he could be. He would have to try out Hywel's way of 'asking God who to help', although he wasn't exactly sure how He would know when God answered him! Another thing he had yet to learn.

'I can still sing, though, even if I haven't got the other type of worship worked out yet?' he asked Hywel teasingly.

'Yes, you can sing, but please don't ask me to join in; that would scare the birds from the trees.' Hywel laughed as he closed his eyes to the setting sun.

Beloved friends, what should be our proper response

to God's marvelous mercies?

I encourage you to surrender yourselves to God to be

his sacred, living sacrifices.

And live in holiness, experiencing all that delights

his heart.

For this becomes your genuine expression of worship.

Romans 12:1, TPT

7
Peace

Before the sun had risen, Hywel and Philip were up and had the horses laden. It was a dull, overcast day and the air was damp, with a fine mist rolling in from the sea. They had both woken chilled, while it was still dark, and worked in silent agreement to hastily pack up their camp. As they rode down into the town, doors and windows were beginning to open, and there were already a few people milling around in the harbour area. Hywel pulled up and dismounted on the quayside. There were two large ships in the harbour, and several smaller vessels.

'I'll go and make enquires and see if either of those cargo vessels are going our way,' Hywel handed Philip the reins of the horses. Philip dismounted and tied the four horses to an iron ring on the low stone wall that separated them from the swirling muddy water below. The horses were agitated with all the unfamiliar sights and sounds of the port: the noise of the ships' rigging rattling, the seagulls screeching. There were more people about now too, as the rising sun lightened the dawn sky. There was shouting and banging as the morning's work and trading began. Philip soothed the horses as best he could, with a few soft words and a handful of oats each from his saddlebag supply. He sat down on the wall, not sure how long he would have to wait for Hywel to return.

He heard the soldiers approach before he saw them. The familiar sound of sword clinking against chain. He glanced up. There were two of them. He didn't think he recognised them, but he knew his face was well-enough known and his reputation more so. A frisson of fear went through him. Would they recognise him? He ducked his head, and quickly pulled his hood up to cover his face. He was thankful that the horses stood between him and them.

'That's a fine-looking horse.' One of the soldiers spoke, but Philip didn't think he was addressing him. He was admiring Noble but in conversation with his companion.

'Fine, indeed. Make a good fighting horse, although looking a bit past his best, perhaps?'

Noble was hanging his head and Philip could swear he was trying to look pathetic.

The second soldier stepped close and tried to take hold of Noble's reins, but the great horse was too quick for him and shook his head violently so that he missed his grip.

'Ha! Feisty, too, I see. I knew and admired a horse much like this one once before. I saw Philip de Braose astride a destrier very like this one and remember being jealous then of his mount. But then, he was a nobleman and a class above me. I could never have afforded such a beast.'

Philip held his breath. How was it that someone would recognise the horse and not him? Perhaps they should have thought to disguise Noble as well as himself? He would laugh about that with Hywel later, if he got through this.

'Whatever happened to de Braose?' The first soldier was speaking again. They had stepped back from Noble but were standing admiring him from a safe distance, still within Philip's earshot. He feigned disinterest, keeping his head bowed and his arms clasped tight across his chest, his fingers white with the effort.

'I heard he had gone rogue, fighting for hire in minor skirmishes all over the south of France. And that he met his end finally in one of those skirmishes,' was the reply.

'So Philip de Braose is dead?'

'So I heard. Although whether anyone mourned his passing I would seriously doubt.' The soldier laughed dryly at that.

'Philip de Braose is dead.' That is what Philip had heard. It hit him forcefully. He slowly let out the breath he had been holding, trying desperately not to draw their attention.

'Good morrow, gentlemen.' It was Hywel's familiar voice, and Philip dared to breathe normally again.

'Fine horse, brother. Fighter, I would guess?' the soldier turned as the monk approached them, acknowledging his greeting.

'Retired, I'm afraid, and coming back to Wales with us to enjoy his retirement with these young fillies here.' Hywel responded lightly, but with an edge to his voice.

'Not for sale, then?' the first soldier asked, stepping forward as if to intimidate the monk into perhaps considering an offer.

'No, I'm sorry to disappoint you, my friends.' Hywel stood tall, resolute and unmoving.

'Well, good day to you, brother.' The soldier reluctantly backed away and nodded resignedly at Hywel, adding, 'And to you, brother,' in Philip's direction. He had been noticed, then? Philip stayed as he was, only dipping his head slightly in response.

'They have gone.' Hywel spoke a minute or two later.

'Thanks be to God!' Philip pushed his hood back just enough to be able to see Hywel's face, but kept it up, covering his head. It felt safer that way. But he wouldn't be recognised now, would he, if he were thought to be dead?

'Did you hear what they said about me?'

'Yes, apparently you are dead.' Hywel was matter of fact.

'It was a shock to hear it. I don't know quite what to make of it. Should I be pleased?' Philip really was unsure how he felt about the news of his own death. There was definitely a certain finality about it.

'Well, I think the Philip de Braose you were needed to die, but who is to say if God will not restore you to the version of Philip de Braose He created you to be? In the meantime, I think you must get used to living in your new identity.'

'As Brother Robert?'

'Yes, and as a son of the Most High God.' Hywel glanced over at him. All the time he had been talking he had been busy untying and soothing the horses.

'Did you get us passage?' Philip forced his thoughts back to the matter in hand.

'I did. That vessel there,' Hywel pointed to a large ship that was being loaded with oak barrels and casks, 'is bound for Bristol on the midday tide. The captain has agreed to take us and the horses for a reasonable price. He made some comment about making sure we were no "Jonahs", but I think he was joking.'

Hywel's normal smiling face was pensive, anxious even, Philip thought.

'We can load the horses at any time,' Hywel continued.

Philip's stomach rumbled. 'Could we stop for some provisions first?'

'Well, you can, by all means,' Hywel grimaced slightly, and his face seemed a little paler than normal.

They found a pie shop and Philip enjoyed the savoury pie so much that he purchased another for the journey. Hywel stood a distance away while he ate, studying the ship they were to travel on.

'Looks solid enough,' Philip laughed, nudging Hywel out of his reverie.

'Yes.' But the monk was not laughing with him. Philip saw a look of determination appear on Hywel's face.

'Come. Let us get these horses aboard,' he said. He added in a whisper, 'I will do it, even if afraid,' so low that Philip almost missed it.

They led the horses up onto the deck of the huge ship and down a ramp that the sailors had used to roll the great wine casks into the hold of the ship. Hywel seemed to be fussing more than usual over the horses.

'I am sure they will be fine,' Philip said lightly. 'Noble has travelled across water many times, and we have oats for them and there is fresh water aboard, I'm sure.'

'Yes.' Hywel was definitely less communicative than normal. He stepped back from the horses. 'I am going back ashore for a while. I will return before she sails.'

Hywel made a hasty retreat back up the ramp and down off the ship. Philip watched as he hurried down the quayside and then realised where he was heading. There was a stone-built church with a fine square bell tower at the far end of the street. Hywel disappeared inside. Philip smiled to himself. So the man was scared of the sea? He was glad in a way that Hywel suddenly seemed a lot more human. Philip turned his attention back to the horses, and found an open barrel with some water and a dish that he could use to water both himself and them.

By the time the ship sailed out of the harbour, the fine mist had developed into a persistent rain, and the breeze had strengthened, which was good for the sails. The brothers had been encouraged to stay below and make themselves as comfortable as possible, while the sailors above did their job of getting them out of the harbour and into open sea. By the rolling of the ship, and the drips of rainwater falling through the gaps in the deck above their heads, Philip thought it probably best they stayed below anyway. He had settled down with his back against a support post. Hywel, across from him, had done likewise. Hywel groaned. He had turned very pale, with a decidedly green tinge to his face.

'Oh, my friend. Not a good traveller, then?' Philip scooted over to Hywel's side with a dish of water but the monk turned his head away.

Unfortunately the gentle rocking of the ship became much more pronounced as the ship left the relative safety of the bay and turned to sail around the headland of Bretagne and into open sea beyond. The ship was rolling and lurching as the wind picked up and the sea responded, with waves thumping noisily against the sides of the hull.

The long hours sailing across the open sea were miserable for Hywel. He had emptied his already empty stomach and lay curled up on the floor, groaning occasionally. Even Philp felt it a bit, regretting slightly that pie he had broken his fast with, and definitely not wanting to eat the one waiting for him in his saddlebag. But he was a much better traveller than Hywel, and busied himself keeping the horses as calm as he could. At one point a young sailor ducked down into the hold, carrying a stoppered leather jug.

'Here, this might help to settle your stomachs. It's the best Bordeaux wine. We might have had to open a cask or two and put it down to storm damage.' He grinned sheepishly. 'It's a rough one, to be sure, but it will calm again once we have made it around the Cornish headland and into the great river channel.' He nodded once and scooted back up the ramp.

Philip drank from the jug gratefully. It really was very, very good wine. He smiled. Storm damage? He was pretty sure that no cargo of wine made it fully intact from Bordeaux to Bristol, whether the trip was stormy or not. A little bonus for the sailors, he guessed, and probably overlooked by those who paid them. He tried to get Hywel to sit up and take a sip, but the monk was not responsive. Philip could make out a whisper from time to time. He was likely praying. Philip sat down beside him and prayed silently with him. He could do that much for his friend.

He wasn't sure how many more hours had passed, but Philip came to, out of a wine-warmed doze, to realise that the ship was not moving up and down nearly so much. The deck was almost level beneath them; the only indication that the ship was still moving was the gentle roll from side to side. Hywel had also fallen into a fitful doze, but his more from exhaustion, Philip guessed. He shook him gently and proffered the wine jug.

'Here, if you can take some of this, I think it will help. It seems the worst of the storm has passed.'

Hywel gingerly raised himself up into a sitting position. He still looked very pale and there was a fine sheen of sweat on his forehead. He took the jug from Philip's hand and sipped it tentatively. He closed his eyes and lay his head back against the post.

'Good wine,' was all he could manage.

'I'm going up on deck to see how things are. The horses are fine.'

Hywel nodded slightly in reply. His hand was still gripping the jug around its neck. Philip hoped he would avail himself of some more of the wine.

He returned within minutes. 'We are in the river channel and it is much calmer. The clouds are clearing and the sun is appearing too. The sailors think you would do better above deck now, where the air is fresher and you can focus on the horizon.'

Hywel allowed Philip to help him gently to his feet, and they staggered in rather an ungainly fashion up onto the deck. Philip helped the monk to sit down, his back resting against a huge barrel. He handed him back the wine jug.

'Thank you, my friend. It makes a change for you to have to care for me.' Hywel actually managed a small smile up at Philip.

Philip stood by him, his hands on the deck rail looking out to sea. 'You can see land just on the horizon now. Wales,' he breathed.

'That's good. That's very good,' Hywel replied with feeling.

'I'm sorry that you suffer so much from the seasickness.'

'I am too. I've prayed many times that God would miraculously cure me of it.'

'But you travel across the sea regardless?' Philip wondered why Hywel hadn't told him before they sailed that this was likely to happen. There was still much for him to learn about this man.

'Sailing is a means to an end. Worth it, usually. Although that was a rough crossing,' the monk replied grimacing.

'It is good for me to see that you aren't perfect,' Philip smiled down at him.

Hywel snorted. 'Oh, my friend, I am far from perfect, and you will discover that soon enough! There was only one man who walked this earth who was perfect.'

'Jesus?'

'Yes.' Hywel still wasn't at the talkative stage, obviously.

'Jesus didn't have seasickness, then? Philip teased.

'He slept peacefully through a storm.'

'Yes, I remember that story.' Philip wasn't completely ignorant of the Gospels, especially the stories that had been told to him as a child. 'The disciples were terrified and thought they would drown. Didn't they wake Jesus and He got up and stilled the storm?'

'Yes.'

'I wonder how it was possible for Him to sleep through what caused those seasoned fishermen abject terror?'

'Peace.'

'Yes I remember. He spoke, "Peace, be still!"[4] to the wind and waves.'

Hywel looked up at Philip. 'Jesus carried peace and so could speak what was in His heart already,' he said, before focusing his attention back on the sea and sky, as if he were willing them to stop moving up and down.

Philip could see that they were approaching the end of their journey; the hills of Wales were clearly visible, and the ship had slowed to almost a snail's pace, as it negotiated the narrowing waterway, letting the tidal waters draw them in. Hywel was looking a little flushed now and had put the wine jug down.

'I don't think I should drink more of that until I can line my stomach with food,' he smiled weakly. He heaved himself up to stand a little unsteadily next to Philip at the ship's rail.

'I would agree, brother, you are rolling almost as much as the boat did,' Philip jested, while grasping Hywel's arm to help him steady himself. They stood watching together as the ship came smoothly into harbour.

The port at Bristol was as busy and bustling as Bordeaux had been. The sun was low in the sky as they disembarked, the horses seemingly as grateful for solid ground under their feet as Hywel obviously was. They found a baker selling off the last of his day's bread and sat on a grassy bank to eat it, finishing off the jug of wine the sailors had insisted they keep. Two small

---

[4] Mark 4:39, NKJV.

casks of the fine wine were also tied to the horses' backs. Hywel had paid fair price for those, though.

'We might have to sleep under the stars again tonight,' Hywel said. 'We need to catch a ferry boat across the river, but I think I've done enough boat travel for one day. And I think a night in the fresh air is what I need more than anything.' They led the horses away from the main buildings of the town and rode north along the track skirting the river shore until they found a small wooded copse slightly back from the water's edge.

'Perfect,' Hywel said, and was quickly making himself and the horses comfortable for the night.

Later, as they lay looking up at the stars through the branches of the trees, listening to the river lapping gently on the shore and to the horses munching contentedly close by, Philip sighed.

'Now, this is peace. It's amazing how the things around us can either make us feel at peace inside or can steal our peace. Storms without can cause storms within.'

'It is true,' Hywel replied. 'The kind of peace I want more and more is the kind that Jesus had, that He promises can be ours. A peace that stays true despite our circumstances.'

'The peace that Jesus experienced during that storm; how do you think He came by that?' Philip was keen to know the answer. Was that kind of peace available to him, he wondered?

'Several things, I think. It was a gift from God, obviously, but I believe Jesus accessed it by His own will. He trusted God to protect them. He knew enough about God's plan for His life to know that it wasn't His time to die, and also that God had a reason for wanting Him on the other side of the lake. He had a God-designed destiny, and a God-arranged destination, and an appointment with a demon-possessed man needing to be freed. He also knew who He was, and that He had the God-given authority to calm the storm. He chose to believe in those things, and not the evidence to the contrary that the storm seemed to present.'

'So,' Philip thought out loud, 'inner peace comes from faith in God.'

'Yes, I would say so. We choose to have faith in who God says He is, and what He is capable of. We can also take courage from who He says we are, His sons. We can trust that He has plans for our lives, and He has the power to accomplish those things for us.'

'Were you afraid on the ship?'

'Honestly? Yes. Fear in itself is a normal human reaction. You would expect to feel fear every time you entered a battle?' He glanced over at Philip, who nodded in response. 'I was afraid, but I have learned to do the things God requires me to do, even when I feel fear. He promises to ride the storm with me, every time.' He continued, 'I prayed the whole time that God would help me, to not let my fear become greater than the faith I had in Him to keep us safe. My mind was eventually able to find a degree of peace, unlike my stomach.' He smiled wryly.

'Why do you think God hasn't cured you from your *mal de mer*?'

Hywel laughed out loud at that. 'Perhaps it's His way of keeping me humble and dependent on Him, and aware of my own frailties. A reminder to me that I am not perfect!' He turned over onto his side, away from Philip. 'Now sleep, my friend. I don't know about you, but I am exhausted and we have a long day ahead of us tomorrow.'

Philip watched the stars for a while until he too felt the pull of sleep. He turned over and was soon breathing peacefully.

I leave the gift of peace with you – my peace.

Not the kind of fragile peace given by the world, but

my perfect peace.

Don't yield to fear or be troubled in your hearts –

instead, be courageous!

John 14:27, TPT

Do not yield to fear, for I am always near.

Never turn your gaze from me, for I am your faithful

God.

I will infuse you with my strength

and help you in every situation.

I will hold you firmly with my victorious right hand.

Isaiah 41:10, TPT

8

Grace Dieu

They started out early again, both having slept remarkably well, and made their way to the small village of Aust, where the ferry ran from one side to the other of the great River Severn. The early morning was bright and clear, and the short boat crossing was uneventful. Hywel was especially grateful for that. They stopped briefly as they reached Chepstow on the Welsh side to break their fast, purchasing some freshly baked bread, cheese and milk. They sat admiring the town's magnificent castle buildings as they ate.

'Impressive.' Philip nodded at the fine stone buildings looming above them, perched as they were on a cliff overlooking the river.

'Yes, definitely makes a statement. Is it to keep the Welsh in, or the English out, do you think?' Hywel smiled over at him.

'Bit of both, probably!' Philip laughed in reply. He added, 'I think I've been here before. I have a vague memory from my youth.'

'You might find you will be passing through places that you are definitely familiar with as we head north, some de Braose lands, even. Are you at peace with that?' Hywel looked pointedly at him.

'Yes. It just feels so good to be back in Wales. Even though I'm not a true Welshman, it feels like coming home.'

'*Hiraeth.*'

'Excuse me?'

'The Welsh call the way you are feeling "*hiraeth*", the earnest longing or desire to be in your homeland,' Hywel explained, grinning.

'I like that,' Philip answered thoughtfully.

'Are you still worried you will be recognised?'

'It is many years since I left here, and I was a barefaced boy then. I may be barefaced again,' he rubbed the stubble on his chin, 'but my face is older and more life-scarred, and I think the monk's disguise will work. I'm unlikely to come across anyone who knew me well enough in my past life to recognise me as I am now.'

'As to your new identity,' Hywel nodded at his habit, 'as we journey through Wales we must necessarily visit some Cistercian abbeys, and may even have to stay at some. I will protect you as much as possible, as you are not yet fully accustomed to our way of life. I must advise you to say very little and follow my lead in all things if you want to play your part well, so as not to arouse suspicion that you are not what you claim to be.'

Philip nodded in agreement. 'I will put my trust in you, brother.'

They left Chepstow following the route of the majestic River Wye, as it flowed wide and slow between steep, densely wooded valley sides. It was a glorious ride, the river water sparkling in the sun, and the air cool enough to keep them and the horses comfortable. Once or twice they had to negotiate their way through tall trees, or down steep paths, but the way was clearly marked as it led them to Tintern. The tall double-storey Abbey church stood proud, with its familiar cruciform structure, built on the meadow flats close to the river shore. Philip could also make out stone-built, uniformly arranged monastic buildings attached to the far side of the church. It was an attractive abbey set in equally lovely surroundings. He was impressed.

'The Cistercians really know how to pick their locations!' he said.

'Yes, Tintern is certainly blessed in where it is located. It is also a well-established and very busy abbey. There will be many eyes watching us, Brother Robert.' Hywel's use of his new name was a timely reminder of the challenge to maintain his new identity. 'I have letters from France for the abbot here, and as it is nearing the time for dinner, I suspect we will be invited to eat with the brothers. I will make our excuses to leave as soon as we can, as we still have some miles to cover today. We stop tonight a few miles north of here at the Abbey of Grace Dieu. That is a very new community and very small. It should be easier for you to play your part there.'

Hywel had been right. After he had spent a few minutes with the abbot in his private lodgings, the two of them had been invited to stay to eat in the refectory. Evidently the abbot had accepted Hywel's explanation about having to be on his way soon after. Philip said nothing for the whole time they were there which, as the community ate in silence, was not too difficult. He nodded and smiled along with the other brothers as food was passed down the table. If the abbot had asked after him, Hywel didn't say. They left Tintern, both they and the horses well fed and watered, and made their way up the river valley towards Monmouth, turning westward to find Grace Dieu.

The Abbey came into view as they crested a small rise. It was a far cry from the splendour of Tintern. Situated on slightly undulating meadowlands that ran along the side of a narrow, muddy river, it consisted of a small, simply built rectangular church and an odd collection of wooden buildings arranged around an open-squared cloister.

'The abbot at Tintern was pleased we were calling in here,' Hywel turned back in the saddle, as they slowed before they made their approach to the Abbey.

'Oh?' Philip pulled up beside him.

'Yes. It is a very new community, only founded in the last few years, and already has an apparently poor reputation among the Cistercians. Every Cistercian abbey community is supposed to be self-governed and self-sufficient, but so much depends on the abbot of each house as to how well that is accomplished. The abbot at Tintern, I think, was hoping I would report back what I find here. Needless to say, I will probably conveniently forget to do so.' Hywel chuckled.

Philip was intrigued now. There was no porter at the door to officially meet them as they entered the open gateway into the Abbey enclosure, leading their horses. A small, rotund monk came hurrying out from the direction of a wooden building. He did not seem all that happy to see them, and did not apologise that they were not welcomed appropriately. He bowed stiffly in an attempt to greet them, but his eyes were wary. He pointed to what could barely be described as a stable, more a lean-to. Hywel and Philip made quick work of settling the horses, and took a moment to carefully hide the two wine casks they had carried with them beneath some straw behind where they had tied Noble. Something felt decidedly odd about this place; they trusted that no one would get past the grumpy old horse to discover their treasure.

The monk was standing waiting for them as they emerged. He turned, obviously expecting them to follow, and wordlessly led them around the cloister and into a long, low building which obviously served as the monks' accommodation. One end was furnished with a long wooden table with benches either side. A single ornate, carved wooden chair stood at the top of the table. At the other end of the long room was a wooden partition, through which the monk led the two guests. This was obviously their sleeping quarters. Six beds were arranged, three along each side wall. Their guide pointed to the two beds at the far end. Hywel nodded his thanks and he and Philip dropped their saddlebags on to the beds. The sun was getting low in the sky so they assumed that the brothers would be returning soon from their work and that the bell would ring for Vespers.

No bell sounded, not at the time for Vespers and not after that. The monks did reappear, one by one, wearing their black scapulars, soiled with the evidence of labour. Before long there were four, including the small monk who had greeted them. He disappeared and returned with a large jug and a plate of wrinkled apples that had obviously been stored over winter and looked decidedly unappetising. He indicated for Hywel and Philip to join them at the table, poured water into beakers and placed them in front of them.

Philip glanced around as surreptitiously as he could at the faces of the brothers at the table. He noted that Hywel was making his own study also, while carefully biting into the soft apple he had been handed. There was definitely something wrong here. The faces around the table were tired, careworn, unsmiling. The atmosphere in the room was palpably miserable. The monks ate in silence.

A noise from outside the door caught Philip's attention. A tall monk rose quickly from the table and Philip watched as he went out of the door and returned helping a stooped monk who was leaning heavily on a stick and shuffling painfully across the room towards them. The abbot sat down heavily in his chair and his companion bowed to him and backed away to reclaim his place at the table.

'Welcome, brothers.' The voice was weak and wheezy. 'We are not used to visitors...' He was interrupted by a violent coughing fit.

Hywel stood to his feet and, bowing slightly, offered him a cup of water.

'Father Abbot, do not exhaust yourself on our account. We are well met.' He spoke softly to reassure him.

The abbot gratefully took a sip and laid his head back against the high back of his chair, raising his hand slightly. At the sign, the small, round monk who had greeted them on arrival rose to his feet and came to the abbot's side. He had obviously been designated to speak for the abbot.

'We are not used to visitors. We will offer you what we have to share, but you must know that it is not much. We are not a wealthy community. Can we,' he glanced back at the abbot, 'ask what the nature of your visit is?' His voice held suspicion.

'We merely need a roof over our heads for the night. We do not want to inconvenience you in any way. We are heading north at daybreak,' Hywel replied respectfully, acknowledging the abbot with a slight bow as he did so.

The deputised monk spoke again. 'Forgive us if we appear unwelcoming.' His voice cracked slightly. 'We have much to contend with here. Not least our concern over our abbot's health.' He was clearly speaking for himself now and not so much for the abbot, who had closed his eyes, exhaustion lining his face.

'Can we be of any assistance to you at all?' Hywel asked quietly, with genuine concern.

'What we need, I fear you cannot supply. I only ask that you not judge what you find here, as others have, or spread false rumours about us. We have enough to contend with, with enemies on our doorstep; we need no enemies further afield.' His face looked grim.

'Would you permit me the honour of explaining to me how it is that things are so difficult for you here?'

Hywel had the extraordinary ability to make people share their deepest concerns, as Philip was well aware. He carried an inherent trustworthiness. It seemed that the monk had assessed Hywel and also judged him so, as he sat down on the edge of the bench nearest the abbot and indicated for Hywel to sit opposite him. The other monks busied themselves. One was clearing the table, the other two were leaving the room with their hoods up. The abbot remained slumped awkwardly on his chair.

'My name is Brother Silas. I came here with my brothers five years ago to form this new community. We were sent from our mother house, Dore Abbey, under the patronage of John of Monmouth. But Dore Abbey is an English house, and we have not been welcomed by the local Welsh. They definitely do not like us being here. We have tried to acquire land for agriculture, and pasture land for sheep. We have been thwarted at every turn; even our sheep have been stolen from us. The local Welsh have raided our stores more than once. We have grown what we can, planting vegetables and small areas of grain where we are able, but it is scarcely enough to feed us. Our abbot is in increasingly failing health, and we are at the end of our endurance. Forgive me, brother.'

Silas hung his head, obviously overcome with emotion, and Hywel gave him time to gather himself before replying, 'None of us can rightly judge another until we have walked the same journey. You will find no judgement here.' He paused until Silas had raised his head so that Hywel could reassure him with his eyes. 'I do ask, however, why we have heard no call to prayer?'

'To our shame, brother, we have abandoned the offices. But not the prayer,' he was quick to add. 'Because of the situation we find ourselves in, we work more hours of the day, we have no lay brothers or locals willing to help us and so we are rarely able to meet together. We celebrate Prime and Compline together, at the beginning and end of the day, but apart from these, we merely leave the doors of the church open so that each of us can make use of it personally, when we can, during the day. I can only speak for myself when I say that my devotion to God remains as strong as ever, but I cannot prove it by rule-keeping.' He paused, looking up at Hywel, who nodded in understanding.

Silas continued, 'Each of the other brothers here must account for themselves. Some have found it hard to pray at all, I am sure. It has felt at times like God has abandoned us. You must know that in addition to missing offices we have abandoned other parts of the Rule also. When you have little to eat, you do not limit what you can eat. We will eat fish and eggs and meat whenever we can get it. I believe it is the reports of these violations that have spread the rumour that we are a disobedient community at best, and immoral at worst.'

Hywel did not respond to this. Meat was usually forbidden for Cistercians, and fish and eggs only permitted on feast days and anniversaries, or to serve to important visitors. He could see how some might have judged them on this, but he had heard no definite rumours and would not add any fuel to that particular fire.

'It will be our honour to pray with you, and for you, at Compline this evening,' he said, smiling sincerely and grasping Silas' shoulder briefly, before rising and taking his leave, nodding at Philip to follow suit. The two of them made their way out into the dusk-lit cloister and back towards the horses.

'Are we leaving?' Philip whispered as they reached the stable. He had heard enough of the conversation to know that their stay here was a potential burden to this small community.

'No. That would be the worst thing we could do, having encouraged them to unburden themselves to us. At best, leaving now would look like ingratitude for their simple hospitality, and at worst would confirm that we were only here to spy on them.'

'But what can we do to help?' Philip knew that was Hywel's heart, and felt a similar pull.

'Very little. I can send letters to counter the rumours, maybe. I need to think and pray on that. I think for the time we are here, the best we can do for them is to pray with them, show them kindness and serve them as we can. Offering them our friendship, and the comfort of our understanding. There is one other thing I think we should do, though?' It was a question as much as a statement.

'What's that?'

'The wine. It was a gift for an abbot friend of mine in another much wealthier abbey, but I would like to leave a cask here for the brothers. They can use some to bolster their abbot's poor health, or maybe sell it for small profit. Either way, it is the best we can offer.'

'That is a generous gift, brother, and I can see how it might benefit them.'

'Bless them, I hope.' Hywel ducked beneath Noble's head and retrieved one of the casks.

The wine cask was placed on the table in the refectory as they left the following morning. Silas accepted it, and the genuine kindness it was offered with. His eyes were moist, but a small smile graced his tired face.

'I will not forget you, brothers.'

'Nor we you,' Hywel replied. 'You will continue to be in our prayers, Silas. Hold on to hope, brother. Your devotion to one another and to God is evident to us. God will hear your prayers, I believe it.' Hywel blessed them as they left.

Philip and Hywel rode away from Grace Dieu with heavy hearts, and for the first few miles in silence.

'I wish we could have done more!' Philip spoke first. His frustration had turned to anger in the time since they had left the Abbey. 'It just seems so unfair, when other abbeys in Wales are doing so well, and have Welsh patronage, that they should be so harshly treated, both by the locals and by some of their other brother communities!'

Hywel kept his horse at its steady pace and replied softly. 'I understand your anger, brother. I too feel deeply moved by their plight, but I have learned to accept that there are some situations that come my way that I can to do very little to help change. We are but two. If we had stayed to help them physically, they would have struggled to feed us alongside themselves. We have no power to change the way the Welsh feel about them, or to fight on their behalf. But we did have the power to encourage and bless them, and we still have the power of prayer. We must trust that God will fight their battles and provide for them. We can also speak up if we hear false rumours and counter them with words of praise – for the dedicated, hard-working and faithful men we have had the pleasure to meet at Grace Dieu.'

'As usual you respond with wisdom and grace, as I get agitated and combative,' Philip conceded. 'I still have much to learn, but I can see that you are right. God must be their saviour, not us.'

'Yes, we can trust their care to the Great Provider and Defender, but not forget the power of our prayers.'

The track they were on was climbing steadily upwards through the trees, surrounded on both sides by the steep incline of the Black Mountains. The horses needed to rest more frequently, and although Hywel seemed keen to keep moving northwards at a reasonable pace, he was responsive to their needs. They pulled up by a stream in a sheltered spot where the trees were thinning. They had very little left in the way of provisions for themselves, but the horses could at least graze for a while, and avail themselves of some fresh water.

Philip and Hywel drank from the stream, and shared the last crust of bread they had carried with them from Chepstow the day before.

'I am trusting that you know where we are going, and that we are making decent progress?' Philip asked as he lay back against a tree trunk, stretching his aching knee out and rubbing it subconsciously. 'The track seems clearly enough marked?'

Hywel smiled in response. 'Yes, yes and yes.' He was sat similarly lounged against a tree with his hands clasped across his midriff. He did not elaborate.

Philip gave Hywel a hard stare. The monk laughed.

'We are heading for Talgarth, where we will find a place to stay tonight, I have no doubt. The path we are following leads us through this valley, and up and over a high pass before we can reach there, but we are more than halfway, and I suspect we will make it before sunset if the weather holds. The sheep traders use this route as do merchants, soldiers, Welsh raiding parties and the odd Cistercian!' He laughed again. 'Beyond Talgarth, our next stop will be the Abbey at Cwmhir.'

Philip registered all that information. 'Talgarth was once briefly in de Braose hands, I believe. My grandfather inherited it through his mother, but King John seized it and gave it to another.'

'That is my understanding too, but it was safer to take this route. Our other alternative was to travel via Hay Castle, and that was much more recently de Braose owned, although as you might be aware, your cousin forfeited that, and his life, by cuckolding Llewellyn.'

'Yes,' Philip sighed heavily. 'You can perhaps understand why I am not necessarily always proud to bear the de Braose name. My relatives have a reputation for making rash and foolhardy decisions and liaisons. I think I will be safe enough in Talgarth, and I agree that Hay might be best avoided if Llewellyn is still on the warpath.'

They sat in silence for a while. Philip wasn't sure he wanted to spend any more time thinking about his ill-fated relatives and their potential legacy. He was glad when Hywel interrupted his musings.

'I have a question for you, Philip.'

Philip glanced over at him. Hywel wasn't looking at him but was twirling what looked like a large buzzard feather in his fingers.

'I'm listening.'

'We have just visited two abbeys, Tintern and Grace Dieu. Tintern was impressive, splendid even, in its construction, situation, size and prosperity. Grace Dieu was humble, ramshackle in places, desperately poor and unwelcoming. From the outside appearance, which would you have chosen to spend the night in, do you think?'

'Honestly? Tintern, probably.'

'Me also. Especially as the Abbey was well run and the Rule adhered to. I would have been able to attend all the offices and keep my vows, and enjoy the lovely atmosphere of the Abbey church. We would have been well served and well rested there. But somehow, I wouldn't change anything. I think now that our stay at Grace Dieu was the more rewarding. We ate little, and slept little. We were treated initially with suspicion and distrust. We missed out on the prescribed offices. But we had the privilege of meeting and spending time with men who were genuinely devoted to God, and to each other, and whose sheer perseverance and determination deeply moved me. They blessed me, Philip, probably as much as we blessed them, if not more.

'One of the things you will learn,' Hywel continued, 'is that the Cistercian Rule is strict and mostly strictly adhered to. Disobedience is not treated lightly. There are some who make it their mission in life to expose those who do not adhere to the vows they have made. In one sense that is acceptable; we need discipline to enable the Order to continue and remain true to its foundational beliefs. But paramount to me is that the life of devotion to God we have pledged ourselves to is helped, and not hindered, by the enforcement of that Rule.'

'Do you believe the criticism of Grace Dieu is right or wrong, then?'

Philip knew Hywel wasn't judgemental, but he was clearly struggling to answer the question.

'That is a difficult one for me. I love the structure of our prayer offices. I baulked at the restrictiveness of them at first, but I came to realise that their purpose was to constantly remind me of what I have been called to. That is, to grow deeper in my knowledge and experience of God, to be totally devoted to Him, throughout my day, whatever other demands are made on my time. It is such a privileged life to be able to spend hours a day in prayer and contemplation. Many outside abbey walls do not have that privilege or capability. But at Grace Dieu, we saw evidence that keeping rules is not always a good indication of a man's devotion to God. Indeed, you will meet monks, I am afraid, who are religious in their pious observance of the Rule but have no living relationship with God to speak of. False piety and religious observance can be a pretence for a heart not truly submitted to God. Jesus called people like that, the Pharisees of His day, "whitewashed tombs".[5] Outwardly appearing clean, but dead and decaying inside.'

'Powerful picture,' Philip said. 'So you are saying, be careful how we judge people from what we observe on the outside? Like the appearance of Grace Dieu not truly representing what was inside?'

---

[5] Matthew 23:27, NKJV.

'Yes, and that as you learn the ways of our Rule, I am hoping that you see the prayer offices for what they are, an aid to help in your devotional journey, and not just a rite to be observed for the approval of others. God is much more interested in the state of your heart towards Him than He is in how well you keep the rules of the Order.'

Philip nodded; he knew abbey life was going to be a challenge for him, and learning its way of life daunting. At least he wanted to start out with the right motivation.

'Saying all of that,' Hywel turned to look pointedly at Philip, 'I expect you to do your very best to learn and follow our ways as much as you can, if you expect to stay inconspicuous among us. It will reflect badly on me if I introduce an apostate into our community at Cymer.'

'I promise you that I will do my very best. I owe you that much. But I admit to being concerned at how much I have to learn in a short time.'

'That's why I am taking you to Abbey Cwmhir first,' Hywel smiled at him. 'I know the abbot there, and between us we can get you looking and behaving more like the Cistercian you are claiming to be. He'll enjoy the challenge. And I'll be grateful for the break from looking after you,' he joked, standing up and kicking Philip lightly. 'Come on, time we were going.' He reached down and grabbed Philip's hand to help pull him to his feet. 'My stomach is telling me that we need to get to the inn in Talgarth as soon as we can. And the smell emanating from you suggests a bath wouldn't go amiss either!'

Philip shoved Hywel playfully. 'Both of us need a bath, I would say. And my stomach out-rumbles yours every time!'

the LORD does not see as man sees; for man looks at

the outward appearance,

but the LORD looks at the heart.

1 Samuel 16:7, NKJV

9
Cwmhir

Talgarth more than met their needs. The inn was well set up, being used to catering for considerable numbers of travellers. It had communal rooms for eating and sleeping that were clean and well furnished. It also had some smaller private rooms, and it was these that Hywel and Philip chose to make use of. The food was fresh and hot, and plentiful. Attached to the inn was a small public bath house, so both brothers were able to avail themselves of a tub of warm water. It felt so good to be able to strip off the grubby, damp tunics and braies they had lived in for so many days. The Cistercian Rule usually barred the wearing of undergarments but made concession for monks travelling on horseback. They were both sincerely grateful for that. A maid cheerfully whisked their soiled garments away and they were laundered and returned to them by the time they left the following morning.

The day dawned bright as they continued their journey, weaving their way alongside the River Wye. The river had rejoined their route, now narrower and faster-moving than it had been lower down its reaches. It tumbled and swirled below them, white water spraying over rocks and glinting in the sunlight. Tall trees stuck their thick roots into the water's edge and small birds dipped and dived for insects. Their ride was harder going, negotiating rocks and trees and inclines and descents, but it was soul food to be able to enjoy God's creation, in clean clothes and with full bellies. It made Philip want to sing out loud, but he restrained himself. The only songs he knew were bawdy songs that he wasn't sure were fit for a monk's ears. He wished he knew how to worship God with his singing voice, but what was it Hywel had said about worship not having to be in song? Philip consoled himself by humming under his breath and thanking God in his heart for the day's good gifts.

They followed the route of the river until they reached the small town of Buellt, where they stopped to water and change horses, and share a loaf of bread they had saved from their generous breakfast at Talgarth.

'How far on is Abbey Cwmhir?' Philip asked, as they ate.

'Not as far in miles as we have come, but as far in time, so we must not linger here,' Hywel replied.

The sun was now at its highest in the sky. Philip trusted Hywel to know where he was headed, but as they left Buellt following the River Irfon, the track was becoming less well marked, and before long they were following winding trails through oak forests, the river below them narrowing to not much more than a stream. They were descending into a valley. Suddenly the trees parted and Philip got his first view of Cwmhir. The Abbey itself was perhaps not as impressive as Tintern, but its location was just as remarkable. It sat on a wide valley floor with rolling hills rising to either side of it, seeming to shelter the Abbey from all intruders. It was if they had entered a private paradise. That was how the Cistercians liked it, seemingly. The Abbey church was a fair size, and the monastic buildings well constructed from stone. The Abbey was obviously blessed with provision from the land, as Philip could see both pastoral and agricultural land marked out and enclosed for some distance around the Abbey conclave.

Philip followed Hywel as he led the way down into the valley towards the Abbey. The sun was beginning to descend and would soon drop below the tops of the hills, and it was obvious Hywel was keen to get there as he spurred his horse to a trot. Philip did likewise, Noble responding somewhat reluctantly. The path they were on widened as they approached the Abbey gate, which was already open, a large monk standing ready to greet them. They reined in and dismounted.

'Brother Hywel, God be praised. It is good to see you! I was informed visitors were approaching, and when I saw monks on horseback, and leading two more, I wondered if it might be you.' The porter stepped forward and clasped Hywel's hand warmly. 'You certainly have a fine collection of horses with you – no surprise there – but who is this?' he asked, nodding in Philip's direction. The monk had a round, jolly face with little squinting eyes that looked to be permanently smiling.

'Brother Rhodri. What a welcome!' Hywel was all smiles too. 'This is Brother Robert, newly come from France.' He glanced back at Philip, who remembered to play his part and stood serenely, his hands clasped in front of him, saying nothing but bowing slightly in greeting.

'Well, come in, come in. We always have room for friends, old and new.'

The porter grabbed the horses' reins from Hywel's hands, and the two monks and four horses trotted behind him as he half-ran, half-waddled back through the gates. He gestured to a young man in lay-brother garb who came and took the reins from Philip's hands.

'Now, you go and get yourselves to the kitchen and I will get these horses seen to for you. Brother Cellarer will find you some sustenance, I've no doubt.'

'Can you inform Father Abbot of our arrival?' Hywel asked.

'I think he knows.' Rhodri indicated towards a window above them with a slight movement of his head. Hywel didn't turn, but Philip could see a tall figure standing with his hands clasped before him. The figure bowed slightly and moved away from the window. Philip couldn't tell if that was a warm welcome or not. But Hywel seemed happy enough to be here, laughing over something else Rhodri had said.

They were sat in the warm, inviting kitchen a few minutes later, with steaming bowls of broth each and a hunk of crusty bread between them, when Rhodri came bustling in. 'Father

Abbot would like to see you when you are refreshed. You know your way to his apartments?'

'I am unlikely to have forgotten,' Hywel grinned in response. 'Thank you, my friend. Don't feel you need to leave your duties to look after us. I am sure we can find our own way around.'

'Yes, yes, of course.' Rhodri was still beaming. 'You will find beds ready for you in the visitor's lodge, and fresh water for washing. I do have a few things that need my attention before sundown so I will leave you to settle in. You have just missed Vespers, but you will join us for Compline later?'

'Yes, of course. We will see you there.'

The interaction between the two was interesting to watch. There was an evident warmth of friendship. Perhaps that was why Hywel had been so keen to come here, Philip thought. Rhodri bowed once and bustled out.

Philip had said nothing since their arrival. He felt safest that way, he was so conscious of saying the wrong thing and potentially exposing his fraud. He had no idea what the community of the Abbey here was like, and how he would be received. But Hywel was obviously comfortable here, so Philip relaxed his guard slightly. They were not completely alone in the kitchen, but the lay brother and cellarer were busying themselves out of earshot.

'Do we need to check on the horses?' Philip whispered, particularly conscious of their possessions – especially the cask of expensive wine – they had left with the horses.

'No need. I trust our horses will have been as well looked after as we have been,' Hywel replied in his normal voice, 'and our possessions will be waiting for us in our lodgings, I've no doubt.' He had a twinkle in his eyes.

'You seem to know this place – and Rhodri?' Philip didn't bother to whisper in reply.

Hywel snorted. 'I ought to know it. I spent a good deal of my adult life here, within these very walls.'

He finished the last of his broth, and sighed with contentment as he pushed the bowl to one side and turned sideways on the bench to face Philip.

'There are some things I think you should know before we go to meet the abbot.' He was smiling, so it wasn't going to be bad news. 'Cwmhir was my first spiritual home. It was here that I came as a novice, too many years ago for me to count. Rhodri and Julian were novices at the same time as I was, and we spent the year of our novitiate generally causing havoc. We were all prone to mischief, or rather Rhodri was, and we couldn't help being led astray. It caused the poor monks here to despair over us at times. But we made it through the probation, and all three of us took our vows and received our tonsure at the same time. I was here for another ten years or so, and loved working with the livestock, but my real skill was with horses. I was frustrated that there were only working horses for me to look after here.

'Abbey Cymer, my home now and our final destination, was founded about forty years ago by a group of monks sent from here. I wasn't here then, I'm not quite that old! But Abbey Cwmhir has always supported the smaller community and provided help when it is needed. When the horse keeper at Cymer passed on, I was asked if I would go. I was sad to leave here, but excited at the challenge it presented – to develop a breeding programme to supply the prince and other Welsh nobles with good horses.'

'So Rhodri stayed, and is porter now?'

'Yes, and almoner. A position with great responsibility. He's come a long way from the red-faced rascal he was when he arrived here!' Hywel laughed.

'And you mentioned another? Julian, was it?'

'Yes, he is still here too. He's the abbot now,' Hywel said with a straight face, but then laughed at the look of consternation on Philip's face. 'Don't judge him until you have met him. He is a good man and devout, and serious about his position here, but he still has a light side. I think you'll like him.'

Philip thought about all that Hywel had said. He felt a little less worried about being here now. There was one thing that intrigued him, though.

'Rhodri is almoner, and Julian is abbot. Does it not bother you that you are only a horse breeder? Did you not have ambition yourself, especially with your connections?' Philip brought to mind Hywel's powerful uncle, Abbot Jerome.

Hywel was thoughtful for a moment but the smile never left his face. He didn't seem offended by Philip's question. 'Maybe I did, once. I might have even thought it was my due, to be rewarded with a position here, or even in a larger abbey. But God had different ideas. I've come a long way since my wild and headstrong days. I have learned a lot about myself, and I am now very content to be exactly where God wants me to be, and exactly all God says I am to be.' He paused, and then laughed again. 'Besides, I never liked books like Julian did. Nor had an aptitude for figures like Rhodri. I much preferred rearing horses to reading or studying. I knew where my natural and God-given talents lay, and where they didn't.'

'I wouldn't limit your talents to horse rearing,' Philip replied with sincerity. 'God has given you great wisdom that I have benefited much from, and great compassion and kindness also.'

'It's taken me a lifetime of learning to get this wise, and a lifetime of mistakes too! But thank you for your kind words,' Hywel replied with a slight grasp of Philip's hand that was resting on the table between them. 'Now we must get to the abbot or he will think we have got lost.' He stood up abruptly from the bench, and waited for Philip to join him.

There was little chance of them getting lost as Hywel was obviously familiar with the Abbey. They found the abbot's apartments on the upper floor of a fine stone building that housed the chapter house below. The knock on the door was answered with an authoritative, 'Come.'

They entered, and the abbot rose to his feet and stepped forward to greet them. He was tall, taller even than Hywel, but much slighter in build. At first glance he had an austere look about him. His tonsure was dark but streaked with grey. His nose was long and his face pale, and his startlingly dark eyes appeared black in the dim light. The window was letting in the last rays of the day's sunlight, but it cast long shadows. The abbot moved over to where a single lit candle was placed on a small table, which was surrounded by three high-backed wooden chairs.

'Well, are you sitting?' The serious face broke into a huge, rather crooked smile.

Although Julian had first presented himself with the contained dignity probably expected of a man in his position, now, in Hywel's presence, he had visibly relaxed. Hywel moved to where Julian was standing by the chairs, but didn't sit straight away. Instead he did the unthinkable, he grabbed the tall man and gave him the most enormous embrace. Julian didn't respond immediately, holding his arms stiff by his sides, but eventually he lifted one hand and patted Hywel lightly on the back.

'Enough, my friend,' he gasped slightly at the onslaught of affection. 'I'm not one of your hunks of horsemeat.'

Hywel released him, grinning.

'And I am supposed to be dignified at all times,' Abbot Julian continued, shaking his head. 'You always were the worst of influences on me!'

'Me?' Hywel laughed as he sat down heavily on a chair. 'It was Rhodri that was the instigator of most of the trouble, I seem to remember.'

'Yes, well,' Julian made a much more dignified descent into the chair opposite. 'I think your memory might be a bit confused. Too much time talking with horses has likely addled your brain.'

Philip had watched this little scene play out, standing quietly in the half-shadows, feeling a bit awkward, as if he were intruding on a private celebration. Hywel hadn't forgotten him, though, and turned to beckon him forward.

'Let me introduce you,' Hywel said. 'Julian, this is Brother Robert, lately come from France.'

Philip stepped into the candlelight, thankful for the dim light, surprisingly nervous. He still wasn't sure that he wouldn't give himself away. He felt Julian assess him by looking him up and down intently.

'Welcome,' the abbot said, eventually. 'Please, sit.' He indicated the empty chair. 'Well, what brings you both to our door, Hywel? Just a stop off on your way back to Cymer, I presume?'

'Yes, and no,' Hywel replied.

'I might have guessed it wouldn't be a straightforward answer,' Julian smiled ruefully.

'We need your help with a little project. I think you are the best qualified to make it a complete success.'

'Enough with the flattery. What is this project?'

'Him.' Hywel waved his hand at Philip.

'Charming as always,' Julian glared briefly at Hywel and then turned to address Philip. 'What is it that I can help you with, my son?'

Philip wasn't sure how to answer. He looked back at Hywel.

'You can trust Julian.' Hywel reassured him. 'Tell him all that you feel you need to. He is not easily shocked.'

Hywel slumped back lazily in the chair and waited for Philip to tell his story. Julian sat upright, his hands clasped serenely in front of him, his penetrating gaze focused on Philip's face. Philip shifted nervously.

'If you will forgive me, Father Abbot, I will not tell you my real name.' He paused and Julian nodded. 'Needless to say, I am not really Brother Robert. I am not "Brother" anything.' He looked at Julian again, expecting to see surprise, but it did not register on the abbot's face.

'Go on,' Julian said, kindly.

'I needed a new identity. I have found a new identity. My apologies, it is not making sense, is it?'

'More sense than you think,' Julian smiled.

118

Philip took a deep breath. 'I needed to play the part of the monk in order to get safely back from France and through Wales. I did not wish to be recognised. But I also wished to change my life, to put my old life to death, as it were. As it is, rumours have come to light that I am actually already dead on a French battlefield. So now I really do not have anywhere else to go, or any idea what to do next, except that Brother Hywel here seems to feel an obligation towards my preservation.'

Julian took all this in. 'Do you have a faith in God, my son?'

'A recently rediscovered one, yes.' Philip could answer that question honestly enough.

Julian rested back in his chair and closed his eyes. He sat in silence like that for several minutes. Philip wasn't sure if he was indicating the end of the conversation, thinking about how to respond, or praying, or maybe all three. After a few moments he opened his eyes and addressed Hywel directly.

'This is highly irregular, brother, and we are risking our reputations and that of the Order if we are discovered to be knowingly allowing a lay man to masquerade as a Cistercian. Was there no other way?'

'It seemed not at the time,' Hywel answered him. 'The decision was made with great soul-searching and prayer. It seemed as if God was directing us down this course. This man here was close to death when God led me to him, but I believe his life means more to God than just a healed body. There is a good reason why he needs to stay hidden among us. He needs to learn to live again, somewhere safe, somewhere where God can keep hold of his attention. For some reason, God chose me to be his helper in this. And I have come to you. To ask you to be my helper in helping him.'

'So you want me to teach him? What, exactly?'

'What you are good at. How to be a good Cistercian. You are more qualified than I,' Hywel grinned.

'Much more qualified, I would say,' Julian huffed. 'How long do I have with him?'

'A few days, a sennight,[6] maybe?'

'Well, let's hope he is a quick learner. You intend to take him on to Cymer with you?' Julian sighed.

'Yes, for a time at least, until God shows us what is next for him.'

'And Prior William, our old friend, will sniff out an imposter in no time.'

'That is my fear, yes. So you will help us?'

'Against my better judgement, perhaps, but yes, I will. I trust you, Hywel, and I trust your relationship with God. And this young man here obviously trusts that too. We must, however, have some explanation at hand for his stay here. Without lying, preferably.'

'You can tell anyone who asks that he is come to Wales from France to help me with the horses, and has heard about how fine a library you keep at Cwmhir, and is keen to learn from you.'

'Well, I suppose that is close enough to the truth. I would hope that I will not be questioned by any for spending time with him. At least, not to my face,' Julian replied.

'You are held in great esteem, you know that. It is very unlikely that anyone will even think to question you.' Hywel was sincere. 'So where will you start with our friend here?'

'With his habit.' Julian paused and looked at Philip. 'It was obvious from the moment you stepped into the room that the clothes you are wearing were not made for you. The tunic is broad enough for two of you and the hem is almost above your knees.' He smiled his crooked smile again. 'I was waiting for an explanation as to who you are and was not surprised to hear you are not who you claim to be.'

Hywel snorted. 'Well observed! As always!'

Julian ignored him and continued addressing Philip. 'Well, Brother Robert you are now, and him you will stay while you are with us. Be prepared for some serious study and a great

---

[6] A week.

amount of self-discipline. I am up to the challenge. Let's hope you are.'

Abbot Julian rose abruptly to his feet just before the bell for Compline sounded. It was uncanny how these monks knew the office hours instinctively. Philip wondered if he would ever train his body and mind to be that aware of the hours of the day. The abbot led the way out of the room and down through the chapter house and into the church. Philip felt the eyes of the gathered monks on him, but kept his focus on Hywel's back, following him and sitting next to him in the choir. He felt the enormity of the whole thing overwhelm him for an instant, but as the plainsong chant began he felt a tangible peace descend, and knew deep down that he would be safe here at Cwmhir.

The Cistercian rhythm of prayer changed with the seasons and being late spring, with lighter, longer days, the monks at Cwmhir had adopted the summer schedule. There were eight offices spread throughout the day, and the majority of the day was spent in prayer. When they were not attending the prescribed communal prayer offices, the monks spent much time in private prayer and contemplation, and *lectio divina*,[7] the study of sacred texts. The day started with Vigils in the night hours, followed by private prayer and then Lauds, and Prime to welcome the sunrise. Philip attended Vigils with Hywel on the first day of their stay at Cwmhir, but from that time on he saw very little of his friend.

The abbot took Philip well and truly under his wing, and he was not wrong when he said the process of teaching him the Cistercian way was going to be a challenge. In the times when the other members of the community were engaged in work or private contemplation, Philip found himself sitting at a small high desk in a corner of the abbot's private room, lit by a window letting in a flood of natural sunlight. On a table sat

---

[7] *Lectio divina* means 'divine reading' and is a traditional, meditative, contemplative approach to reading Scripture.

beside him was a pile of manuscripts, sourced from Julian's fine library.

'You *can* read I assume?' he asked, after indicating where he expected Philp to sit on that first day.

'Yes, Father Abbot,' Philip smiled in reply. 'I received a good education.'

Julian nodded before continuing. 'It is necessary that you assimilate as much information about the Order and the Rule in as short a time as possible. Some things you will learn quickly by observation and imitation, but these I think you should read. I have marked the most relevant passages for your attention.'

He handed Philip a large tome entitled *Ecclesiastica Officia*.

'This describes in fine detail the liturgy and way of life we aim to follow. When you have read that, there are these also, the *Rule of St Benedict*, and *Carta Caristatis*, which outlines the constitutional framework of the Cistercian Order. Both are also important for you to read. I will answer any questions you may have, but would ask you to read more than you speak. I have many other things requiring my attention.' He nodded again with a slight smile and moved away.

Julian spoke and moved with a quiet serenity. He might have shown a more relaxed side with Hywel, but with Philip he adopted his more dignified persona, and yet Philip did not feel uncomfortable with him. He set about reading what he had been instructed to read.

Hours later, it seemed, his eyes were growing heavy and his head was nodding. He had broken off from his study only to attend Terce. His stomach was also complaining. He looked wistfully out of the window, wondering whether Hywel was out there somewhere, enjoying the fresh air and the horses. Julian looked up from his own desk and laughed softly. 'I can hear your stomach from over here, my son. The bell for Sext will ring presently and then you will be pleased to know it is dinner, or *Prandium*, to give it its monastic title. After you have eaten is a time when many of the brothers here have a rest. I suggest you find somewhere outside to take yours, and get some sun and fresh air. Don't go looking for Hywel, though.'

So he can read my mind too, Philip smiled to himself.

He glanced over as the abbot rose to his feet, continuing, 'Hywel has asked to be released from work duties while he is here in order to spend his time alone in prayer and fasting.'

'Probably just thankful for a break from me,' Philip muttered under his breath, but not so quietly that Julian did not hear it.

The abbot smiled kindly. 'Not that, brother. I can assure you. Hywel has a very special relationship with God, and when he has been on the road and busy in the world outside abbey walls, he finds the opportunity to take a day or two, and to be in close communion with God, a necessity. He will come back to you when he has finished doing what he needs to with God. And your horses are being well cared for by the lay brothers here. Although I daresay your fine destrier wouldn't object to a visit from you.'

He turned and led the way out of the room exactly as the bell chimed for Sext.

Philip felt he owed it to both Julian and Hywel to put as much work in as he could, and he read, studied and observed intently. He learned to only speak with the abbot, choosing to hide behind the Rule of Silence at all other times, only smiling and nodding at the other members of the community, who did not seem to question his presence among them, and who mostly smiled and nodded in response. He began to appreciate the quiet, especially the peace inside the church. The church was an impressive space, the nave extraordinarily long and high, with tall arches atop wide columns, clean whitewashed walls and simple geometric decoration. When he had a few free moments, he would find a place in one of the side chapels and just sit in that peace. He felt he could actually feel God's presence there.

More and more, surrounded by the peace of the place, and watching the gentle ways of the monks and their heartfelt observance of the Rule, the other darker memories of another church, and another churchman, began to fade, so that he had to almost go looking for them. The nightmares were far less frequent too. It wasn't that there weren't still places of fear and darkness inside him – he could find them still – but they were not where his mind and soul dwelt. He knew God was doing something inside him and he guessed that this was the other healing process that Hywel had talked of.

Sometimes he took the quiet moments alone in the church to try to recall some of the things Hywel had already taught him; other times he just talked to God, as if He were sitting there with him. He missed Hywel, but God seemed not to mind him speaking to Him in the same way he had spoken to his friend. It felt more natural to him than the prescribed prayers of the liturgy.

On the third day, later in the afternoon, Julian encouraged Philip to take a break. The day was wet and windy, so Philip headed straight to the stable to see Noble. He was standing stroking the horse's great neck when he felt a familiar hand clap him firmly on his shoulder.

'Good afternoon, my friend!'

Hywel. Philip turned and instinctively embraced the monk. Quickly realising how that might have been too demonstrative, he stepped back and dropped his arms awkwardly to his sides.

Hywel looked different. He was relaxed and his smiling face was serene. It seemed as if he was glowing ever so slightly.

'It's good to see you too, my friend, although you are looking a bit pale. Too much book work and not enough horse riding? I suppose that's what happens when I leave you in Julian's care.' He grinned. 'I have just come from him. He tells me you have worked very hard, and he is impressed with how well you have assimilated a great deal of information in a short time. He thinks you are almost ready to be tried and tested at Cymer.'

'Are you worried about taking me there?' Philip had been thinking about that. He was concerned that he would do nothing to blemish Hywel's standing in his own community.

'No. You will probably still make some mistakes, but we will just pass them off as you being from France, or a little slow,' Hywel teased.

'And I thought I'd missed you!' Philip laughed back.

'The weather is clearing. What say you to a gallop on those hills? I've missed these horses more than I have missed your company.'

Philip grunted good-naturedly. 'I suppose a ride, even in your company, would be better than more book work today.'

By the fifth day Philip could bear to study no more. Julian had been patient with him, and very understanding, but even he could see that Philip had reached his limit.

'I think we have done all we can do for now.' He stepped over to Philip's side and closed the book lying open in front of him. 'I think Hywel is keen to get back on the road anyway, and you have worked hard. I am impressed with you, Brother Robert. I think I can see why Hywel is so sure God has more for you. It has been an honour to teach you.'

'I am so grateful to you, Father Abbot, for your wisdom and patience. And to your community that has welcomed me with such kindness. I feel that I have experienced here a little touch of what heaven must feel like, and I am sure that is in no small part owing to your godly leadership.' Philip rose to face the abbot as he spoke.

'We are far from perfect here. If you stayed among us for any length of time you would soon discover our faults, but thank you for your kind words. I am glad that we have been able to serve you in this way,' Julian replied, smiling.

'And I am glad to have had my faith in "men of God" restored by what I have experienced living here among you all.'

'You will find Cymer different.' Julian's face grew slightly more serious.

'How so?' Philip felt he needed to know as much information as possible so that he could prepare himself.

'It is a much smaller community, and everyone has to work very hard and do their part. You will find you have very little free time, and will be expected to work as hard as everyone else. As to the Rule, it is generally kept well. Prior William sees to that. The abbot is less concerned. He is of an age where just to have the title of abbot of a small remote community suits him perfectly. He takes little interest in the day-to-day running of the Abbey, and delegates much to William. The prior is the one who will be most observant of you, I dare say.'

There was a small knock on the door and Hywel's face appeared. 'Did I hear you mention our dear Brother William? Don't worry too much about him. He will only be concerned if you seem to threaten his position. We all get on pretty well together, and he is not so bad when you get to know him. I think you are ready to come and meet my Cymer family now. We shall leave at first light tomorrow. By your leave, Julian?'

He stepped into the room and Julian came to meet him. The two clasped hands warmly.

'Do not be strangers, my friends. You are always welcome here.'

The LORD is my shepherd;

I shall not want.

He makes me to lie down in green pastures;

He leads me beside the still waters.

He restores my soul ...

Psalm 23:1-3, NKJV

10
Stay-a-Little

Philip's heart was heavy as they prepared to leave Cwmhir. Although he had spent much of his time there behind closed doors, there was something about the atmosphere of the place that just made him want to stay longer. He had felt so at peace, so secure there. But he knew that if he stayed, he would have to work for his keep, or else become a drain on the Abbey and its good brothers. And he also knew that this was not where he was destined to stay; his place was with Hywel. The thought of what lay ahead was definitely unsettling him.

Abbot Julian did not come out to fare them well, but Hywel had spent an hour alone with him privately before the sun had even risen. Rhodri, in contrast, embraced them both enthusiastically, and laughingly made sure they had enough provisions for at least three days, even though Hywel insisted they would be at Cymer within two. He clapped Philip on the back soundly as he mounted his horse, and grinned at them both.

'New habit, Brother Robert? Fits you very well!' he laughed.

Hywel growled good-naturedly at him. 'Whatever you think is going on here, Rhodri, you keep it to yourself, old man!'

Rhodri bowed dramatically, still grinning. 'God go with you both, brothers, and protect you on all sides. Do not be strangers here.' He blessed them as they wheeled the horses around to leave.

Hywel, in contrast to Philip, didn't appear particularly sad to be leaving. He seemed keen to get on the road and set off at a steady pace, whistling tunelessly. The skies above them echoed Philip's rather more sombre mood as they too were heavy, with dark clouds obscuring the early morning sunshine. A few spots of rain fell as they made their way out of the valley and away from Abbey Cwmhir.

'Not great weather for travelling,' Philip said grumpily.

Hywel glanced over at him. 'You will find that trying to avoid the rain in this part of Wales, and at this time of the year, is nigh on impossible. It's as good a day as any to travel. At least it's not snowing.'

Hywel was smiling, but Philip couldn't bring himself to smile back. He put his head down, pulling his hood tighter over his head so that it shielded his face, and urged Noble forward. They were climbing steadily upward and the air was definitely getting cooler.

'Could it snow?' he asked. It suddenly felt like a real possibility.

'It has been known at this time of year, and the route we are to take is quite exposed in places, but I think we will be fine.' Hywel had gone back to his whistling and was clearly enjoying the ride far more than Philip was.

'Where are we headed?'

'I am hoping to get to an inn called Stay-a-Little. There is a blacksmith there who is the best and fastest in the region and this horse of mine needs reshoeing. The inn is adequate for our needs for tonight as well.'

'Stay-a-Little. It doesn't sound promising,' Philip grumbled. 'Presumably a place where people don't want to stay long.'

'Ha,' Hywel laughed. 'You'll just have to wait and see!'

The increasingly heavy rain wasn't helping Philip's mood. Even Noble seemed depressed, his head down and swaying from side to side as he sauntered along. They ploughed on through the rain.

Things improved slightly for Philip when they found an abandoned bothy, with enough roof left to keep the rain off, and they could crawl inside into the dry to eat their midday meal. He rested back against the rough stone wall when he had eaten.

'This ale is good,' Hywel drank deeply from a flagon that Rhodri had insisted they bring. 'Here, have some, it will warm your insides.'

'Not as good as a cup full of that Bordeaux wine would be right now,' Philip complained, but he took the flagon. 'Didn't you intend to give the remaining wine cask to Julian?'

'I did, but he insisted I kept it. I explained that we had left a cask at Grace Dieu, and he understood why we had done that when I described their situation to him. He has offered to write some letters on their behalf, asking for aid and putting the false rumours to bed. I am grateful to him, as he has much more authority to do so than I, and more chance of getting a positive response. He also knew that Abbot Thomas at Cymer would appreciate the wine, especially as I am returning with an extra mouth to feed.' He grinned over at Philip. 'It will help soften the blow.'

Philip still wasn't feeling like smiling much. He shifted his position slightly to stretch out his stiff legs.

'I like Julian. He is a wise, kind and good man. He was very good to take me on and be so understanding of my situation. I hope I can thank him properly one day.'

'He felt rewarded enough by the way you responded to his instruction, believe me. It was a joy for him, he reassured me, to help you become more at home in your new identity. He feels as I do, that you have the hand of God on your life, and will want to see you again, I have no doubt. His good wishes and prayers go with us.'

Philip thought for a moment, running his hand over his neatened tonsure, which had received a much-needed trim before they had left Cwmhir. 'At least I look more the part now.' He glanced down at his new habit, which had been made to fit him perfectly.

'And I am sure you will be able to pass yourself off as a genuine Cistercian in the way you behave also,' Hywel added.

'Julian was a good teacher; you have both been good teachers. I hope I don't disappoint you.' Philip had enough self-doubt in that moment to utter those words with genuine feeling.

Hywel didn't respond immediately but looked thoughtfully out at the rain still falling outside.

'You are changing on the inside also, would you say? Not just your mind, but your spirit and soul?'

He didn't turn to Philip for a response, just waited for Philip to speak when he was ready.

'Yes.' It was said quietly. 'I am. It is hard to explain, but it is as if a new man, a new version of myself, has taken over. I am not as fearful or despairing as I was.'

'Just a little miserable at times!' Hywel glanced back at him, his eyes twinkling.

Philip smiled sheepishly then. 'Point taken, brother. Forgive me... I have not been good company today.'

'We all have days when we feel out of sorts – even me. Back to my question, Philip. Can you explain more?'

'Would it make sense if I said it was as if I was learning how to live again, but live differently?'

Hywel nodded his understanding.

Philip continued. 'I don't have the same anger in my heart, the driving need to prove or avenge myself, the guilt, the shame. Those feelings are gone, or if not gone completely, are certainly much less a part of me. I find myself much more at peace, and even hopeful for the future. Although I am slightly terrified as to what it will look like. I think the reason I am feeling out of sorts, as you put it, today, is that we are on the last stage of our journey and Cymer is getting closer. I don't know what awaits me there; how I will find living in community; how long I will be there. And will it satisfy me, or will I feel the draw back to my old life? That is the thing I fear more than anything.'

'You know you have the best guide, and the best teacher, don't you?'

'You? Of course.'

'No, not me, and not Julian. A far more wise and loving teacher.' Hywel was serious now. 'The Holy Spirit, God Himself, and I believe He has come to dwell inside you. It is He who has brought the change about, He who has created a new man inside you, He who will continue to guide, and teach, and direct you as you follow this new path. You do not have to fear what lies ahead for you, Philip, because He has promised to go before you, and prepare the way for you. It is a lot for you to understand at the moment, but I think you will see His work in your life more and more, grow to trust His ways, and hear Him speaking to you in the quiet of your heart.'

'I think I have heard Him already, perhaps,' Philip responded, 'and I think I am beginning to understand. Thank you, brother; yet again you seem to have put into words just what I needed to hear.'

Hywel smiled and heaved himself up, crouching low to exit the cramped space. Philip willed his aching legs to do the same, and followed him out.

'The rain has eased, I think,' Hywel said, as he untied their sorry-looking horses. 'We could rest longer, but I would rather push on so that we can arrive at Stay-a-Little before dark.'

Hywel was right, the rain had more or less stopped and the clouds had lifted slightly. Philip felt himself lighter also. He knew he needed to trust God for what was to come next for him. He would choose hope, as Hywel had taught him, and thank God for what He had already done to turn his life around.

The road they followed was straight and well defined. It had the features of an old Roman road. Philip had had experience of many such roads in his travels, and recognised the signs. It passed through vast swathes of undulating, green pasture land, with a spattering of grazing sheep. It lifted Philip's heart yet more to spot the spring lambs skipping and scurrying across the fields. New life was evident all around them. They were steadily climbing uphill, as the sun was steadily getting lower in the sky.

The signs of human habitation were few and far between, but as they crested a particular hill, Philip spotted smoke in the distance, rising upwards from a cluster of buildings. As they drew nearer, Philip could see that the inn was built low and long into the hillside, with the smithy attached at the far end. It didn't look like much, but Philip was cold and damp and tired, and his knee was aching abominably from being in the saddle all day again.

'Ho, smith!' Hywel surprised Philip with his yell, and Noble skittered.

A huge bear of a man appeared from inside the smithy. He was wearing a battered leather apron, his bearded face was ruby red, and his long hair wet with sweat.

'Ho, monk!' He lumbered towards them and Philip tensed, but then realised that the bear wore a huge grin on his face.

Hywel jumped down from his horse and took the smith's huge right hand in both of his own. 'Samson, my friend, it is good to see you!'

'And you, brother. Come in, come in. Get out of this weather; the rain isn't far off again, I would say.'

'Ho, wife!' Samson boomed in the direction of the inn. A few seconds passed and the smallest woman Philip had ever seen emerged from the doorway.

'Don't you "ho" me, you great beast!' She was covered in flour, and rubbing her hands on her skirts to try to clean them. 'You made me spill the flour all over myself. What's all the excitement about?' If she was cross, it was short-lived when she spotted Hywel. 'Oh, Brother Hywel, it's you! I'm so glad you are here.' She advanced, smiling. She lifted her floury hands to grab his and then apparently thought better of it, and turned back towards the inn door. 'Come in, come in!' She gestured towards the inn. 'We have no other guests and it is warm and dry inside. Samson will see to the horses.'

'And check their shoes?' Hywel asked, glancing up at the smith.

'Naturally,' Samson grinned. 'Won't take me long.'

Hywel and Philip followed the diminutive woman in through the door. She was right, it was beautifully dry and warm inside and there was a delicious smell of freshly baking bread, and of something else savoury, which made Philip's mouth water and stomach rumble audibly.

'Now, brother, sounds like you could eat?' Their hostess smiled at Philip. 'Come, sit yourselves down, here by the fire, so that you can steam-dry a little, and I'll fix some food for you both. Are you going to introduce us, Hywel? No Rule of Silence here, you know!'

Hywel laughed. 'Anwen, meet Brother Robert. He has come from France with the horses, and is bound for Cymer with me.'

'You will love Cymer,' she said, smiling and turning back to the fire to ladle something hot and steaming into bowls.

She placed the stew before them and cut into a large round loaf of bread, which she set down in the middle of the table. 'It is mutton in the stew, Hywel. I won't tell Prior William if you don't!' Anwen nudged Hywel's shoulder as she served him.

'Oh, bliss, Anwen, it has been too long since I tasted your mutton stew. Why do you think I wanted us to stop here?'

This last was directed at Philip, sitting opposite him at the rough table, his head already lowered over his bowl, and the spoon raised to his mouth. Philip looked slightly embarrassed, as he remembered his manners and lowered the spoon again. 'Forgive me. It smelled so good I couldn't resist it.'

'Don't you wait on our account, brother. Eat up. There is more where that came from.' The little lady bustled back to the other end of the table where she had dumped the flour, and began to clear it up. As he ate, Philip observed her as she moved around the kitchen. She was the size of a young girl, but her face showed her to be middle-aged at least. Her hair was tied back under a wimple, but strands of white escaped in places. Her eyes were bright blue, surrounded by deep laughter lines, and her cheeks had lost the plumpness of youth.

Her husband appeared, looming over them all, and pulled up a stool to join them at the table. He seemed to fill the room all on his own. Odd couple, Philip thought to himself. Samson was huge but also not as young as Philip had first thought. He carried muscle and bulk enough, but on closer inspection his beard and hair were more grey than dark, and his face bore the tell-tale marks of a life hard lived.

'I replaced the shoes on your horse, Brother Hywel, but the other horses seemed to be well enough shod.'

'Thank you, my friend. Told you he was quick,' Hywel smiled at Philip before turning back to Samson. 'Can we impose upon you further and stay the night?'

It was Anwen who replied. She had come to stand beside her husband, her tiny hand resting on his broad shoulder. 'It is no imposition, and you know that, brother. We are an inn, after all, and you are our only visitors, so make yourselves at home here. More stew, Brother Robert?'

Philip was distracted, busy contemplating the empty bowl in front of him. Her words made him jump slightly. 'I would be most grateful,' he said, embarrassed again, as she stepped over, laughing, to refill his bowl. 'It is the best I've eaten for a very long time. Thank you kindly.'

Later that evening, when they had been shown into a space behind a solid wooden partition, with two simple but clean beds, Philip lay back and stretched his aching legs out. He sighed deeply. 'I know I didn't want to leave Cwmhir today, especially in the rain, but stopping here has made it more than worth it. I might just want to stay here and eat like that forever.'

'You'd end up the size of Samson if you ate like that every day for the rest of your life!'

They laughed, then Philip asked what he had been dying to know all evening: 'You greeted them like old friends?' He turned on his side to face Hywel, who was sat on the edge of his bed, his hands clasped loosely before him.

'They are old friends, and very dear ones. I try to call in to see them any time I am passing this way.' He paused, and Philip lay back, thinking that was all the information he was going to get. He could feel the pull of sleep. Then Hywel spoke again and

Philip forced his eyes back open. 'Samson is not his real name. No one knows what it is, although I believe he is a natural-born Welshman. Samson was a nickname, and it stuck. He was a soldier once, like you, and like you I think he experienced things he found hard to forget. He came through here one day, to stay as we are staying, and he never left. Anwen's father was still alive, and needing help to keep the place running. Samson knew how to work the forge and he needed a new life, and Anwen had something to do with him staying too, I'm sure. They have made a good life for themselves here, serving the needs of many travellers and getting quite a reputation for both his skills as a smith and her hospitality. But their lives have not always been easy.' He paused. 'I want to tell you more, but you must know that what I tell you now is not for the retelling. You will understand why.' He waited until Philip nodded his agreement.

'Samson and Anwen desperately wanted a child, but were both older than the usual childbearing age. Anwen did find herself with child, but the child came early and did not survive. She carried five more times, and buried a child each time, before despair set in. I came here around the time they had just buried their sixth child. They were so grief-stricken. I sat with them, and cried with them, and prayed with them. They had given up hope, but I did what I could to bless them. Nine months later, Anwen gave birth to a healthy son. She didn't come away unscathed, and they fought to keep her alive, but the child flourished, and bit by bit she willed herself back to health, so as to be the mother she had always longed to be. Those were the happiest of days for them. Their son grew healthy and strong, and tall like his father, but gentle like his mother.

'I visited here the year the boy turned sixteen. He confided in me then that he felt the call of God on his life and wanted to return with me to Cymer as a novice. I was pleased for him, but so worried for Samson and Anwen. He was their only child and meant so much to them. Could they bear for him to leave them? But this is where they showed their true worth and bound me even closer to their hearts. They had guessed already that Pedr was not meant for the blacksmith's forge, nor for innkeeping. He was a hard-working, obedient and loving boy, but just made for a different life from what they could offer him. They told me that it was their greatest joy to give their son back to the One who had given him to them so miraculously. They wept as we left together, but their joy was also genuine.

'You will meet Pedr soon. He is now a full brother at Cymer. He has the most remarkably pure singing voice, and is our cantor. He has also inherited from his father the ability to design and engineer, to create with his own hands, and you will see at Cymer the results of his ingenuity all over the Abbey. Samson and Anwen travel up to visit twice a year, once in the summer and once around New Year, if the weather permits. They could not be prouder of the man their son has become.'

Philip was deeply moved by the story. 'Remarkable people.'

'Yes. They could have let tragedy and heartbreak define them. They could have believed that they deserved to cling to the son they had fought to bring into the world. They could have fought back at God, and taken offence at Him for wanting their son. Instead they have shown only unconditional love, humility and grace. They epitomise God to me. Much more than many so-called men of God I have known.'

Philip thought for a few moments before speaking. 'I see God in you, and you see God in them. So it seems that God teaches us a lot about Himself through the characters and actions of other people?'

'Yes, it is one of God's favourite ways of revealing Himself. Perhaps one day you will be the means of revealing the character of God to someone else who needs to know Him for themselves.' Hywel lifted his legs up onto the bed and turned over. 'Now, sleep, brother,' he mumbled. 'You have a big day tomorrow.'

Philip closed his eyes but sleep was not as close as it had been. He took the time to pray, thanking God for the people He had used to teach him. For Hywel, Julian, Samson and Anwen. And then asking for the grace to one day perhaps be just a fraction of what they were, to somehow be able to influence the life of someone else, and point them to God.

And I will ask the Father and he will give you

another Savior,

the Holy Spirit of Truth, who will be to you a friend

just like me –

and he will never leave you.

The world won't receive him because they can't see

him or know him.

But you will know him intimately, because he will

make his home in you and will live inside you.

John 14:16-17, TPT

Let every activity of your lives and every word that

comes from your lips

be drenched with the beauty of our Lord Jesus, the

Anointed One.

Colossians 3:17, TPT

11

Cymer

They rose before sunrise and took their leave, not staying to break their fast, still feeling well fed from their supper the night before. Samson and Anwen came to stand together to wish them farewell. Philip glanced back as the horse party approached a ridge that would take them out of sight of the smithy. The couple were still standing where they had left them, so he raised his hand in a final wave. It was a reluctant parting for both parties, it seemed. Hywel spurred his horse on to a steady trot, and Philip did his best to keep up with him on a reluctant Noble.

'Keen to get there, brother?' Philip pulled alongside him as they both slowed to negotiate a stream crossing.

'The route we must take today will get hard for us all to navigate, and will slow us down considerably. So while the going is relatively easy, I would like us to make a good start,' Hywel replied, before picking up speed again.

They had left the main track and were riding more or less across country. Thankfully the weather was dry, and the early-morning sun was warming them nicely. As the day drew on, Philip understood Hywel's plan. The terrain began to change the longer they rode; gradually the gently sloping grass became steeper rocky inclines. Both horses and riders had to concentrate more closely on foot placement, and watch for loose stones. Sometimes they had to wind through dense woodland, other times they had to negotiate narrow cliff-edge paths, but always steadily climbing upwards. The sun was high in the sky now and Philip was grateful for that, as the air was definitely much cooler.

'We are blessed with the weather today. It can get wild up here, and when the mists descend it can be especially treacherous.' Hywel had read his mind.

'Yes. Good that we can at least see where we are going, with all these sheer drops. Am I right in assuming you *do* know where we are going?'

Hywel only laughed as he pulled ahead again.

They stopped briefly to water and change the horses and grab something to eat. Philip could see the peaks of the mountains rising now all around them. It was breathtakingly beautiful and slightly ominous all at the same time.

'Are there Welsh raiding parties around here?' It felt like there could be bandits at any turn.

'Always a risk, but these mountains well and truly belong to Prince Llewellyn now, and most of the Welsh are loyal to him. I carry this as protection.' Hywel reached into his saddlebag and held out a round seal to show Philip. It bore Llewellyn's mark.

'Will our habits not protect us?' Philip asked as they remounted.

'Not necessarily. The Church is held in suspicion by many here, and seen as an easy target, especially as we are believed to have wealth while many locals struggle to even feed their families.'

They rode on, deep in concentration, as the path reached its zenith and then started to wind downhill again. Only when the ground beneath them evened out a bit did they relax into a steady, measured walk to give the horses a break. As the path widened, Philip pulled alongside Hywel.

'Will you tell me more about Cymer? I would like to be as prepared as possible.'

'We are a small community and not a wealthy one, although not as destitute as Grace Dieu. The Abbey is not huge but we have good stone-built accommodation now, and the church is a fine building by my estimation. We have some land for agriculture and pasture, but it is limited by the terrain, although we do run our own small farm. We are self-sufficient, and have spare to help out some of the needy around us, but you won't find stores of treasure in our storehouse. Most of the wealth that we do make comes from the horse breeding, supplemented by sheep wool, and lambs. Cistercians favour the simple life, without ostentation of any kind. We live simply, eat simply, dress ourselves simply, worship simply. We have no need for great wealth.'

'And the people? Who will I be living among?'

'We number only eleven brothers, including Abbot Thomas. You will make it twelve. We have four lay brothers who also live and work among us. We do not tend to have novices; an exception was made for Pedr, because of our connection with his family. So we are a small community, but we work well together, and we work hard also. Every brother has more than one responsibility within the community, and all tasks are shared to ease the burden as much as is possible. I will not describe all the brothers to you by name, as I wish you to meet them and get to know them for yourself. The best way to do that, and to be accepted among us, is to work alongside us. If you show yourself willing to serve in whatever way you can, you will find that you are embraced as one of us much sooner. You will also get to know the brothers for who they really are, as working with them is the only time you will be able to speak with them.'

He paused to navigate a narrowing in the track, before continuing. 'Your main responsibility, of course, will be to help me with the horses, but you must also be prepared to do *all* that is asked of you, and more besides. You will have to turn your hand to many things: shearing sheep with Huw, tending to David's beehives, helping Pedr to construct a dam to divert a stream, peeling vegetables for Aldred, maybe even milking the goats…' He glanced over at Philip and they shared a smile.

Philip was eager to see the place now and, although still anxious, he knew the sooner he entered the world of Cymer, the sooner he would learn its ways. He didn't have long to wait. Within the next hour they had descended a steep hill which levelled out alongside a wide, shallow, slow-moving river. Steep wooded hillsides surrounded them, and just ahead, through some trees, Philip caught his first glimpse of Cymer. He saw the church first, a simply built stone rectangle, but rising to double-storey height above the other buildings that made up the Abbey. To the southern side of the church was what Philip presumed to be the cloister, with its small gatehouse positioned centrally along the western wall.

It was lovely. Not imposing like Tintern, or surrounded by swathes of verdant green like Cwmhir, but striking enough in its own right. The trees and hills and river seemed to enclose the Abbey like an embrace, shielding it on all sides; like it was a hidden treasure just waiting to be discovered.

They approached, crossing the river over a sturdy wooden bridge. It was late afternoon and there were few signs of life. Hywel led the way past the cloister gate and the front of the church. They dismounted and led the horses along the northern side of the church and beyond, where Philip was surprised to find an extensive stable complex, with well-built wooden stabling and a good-sized exercise yard.

'I think we have arrived during Vespers, which is why we were not greeted. Either that or they saw it was me coming and didn't bother.' Hywel laughed quietly, as they led the horses into the stables and set about unloading and rubbing them down. Before long they were joined by an amiable lay brother, who bowed a silent greeting to Hywel and proceeded to take over feeding and watering the horses for them. Hywel said nothing in reply but touched the man lightly on the shoulder and smiled at him as they left the stable.

They approached the rear of the cloister, and entered through a narrow doorway that led to a short corridor that brought them out into the cloister square, alongside a large windowed room that was presumably the chapter house. Then they were spotted. A tall, fair-haired monk with startling blue eyes came towards them with his hands outstretched. His eyes were Anwen's, and his warmth of greeting sealed his identity.

'Brother,' it was barely a whisper. 'It is good to have you safe home.' He was grasping Hywel's right hand in both of his. He said no more but his eyes held a question that Hywel could happily answer.

'They are well, brother. Very well,' he whispered back.

Hywel released himself from Pedr, and smiling, he indicated for Philip to follow him. He led him through another doorway into a large rectangular room that was obviously some kind of a day room, furnished with writing desks and benches. At the far end was a wooden stairway which led above to the monks' sleeping quarters. The upper room was a large dormitory, divided into cells by wooden partitioning. Hywel said nothing but indicated a space for Philip which contained a narrow bed, a small table and an even smaller window.

Philip dropped his few possessions on the bed, and turned to find himself facing not Hywel, but a much smaller, dark-tonsured monk with an unreadable expression on his face. Disconcertingly, his eyes were scanning both Philip and the things he had just dropped on the bed.

'Brother?' It was as much a challenge as a question. His voice was surprisingly high-pitched, almost a squeak, and Philip suppressed the need to laugh, although he was nervous enough to giggle like a silly girl.

'Prior William.' Hywel reappeared just in time. He threw Philip a warning glance, and Philip composed his face into a mask of serenity. 'May I introduce to you Brother Robert, come lately from France, a horse lover and a welcome addition to our little family here?' Hywel didn't give the prior time to contradict him. 'Is the abbot able to receive us? I have a gift for him from Bordeaux.' He indicated the cask in his hands.

William looked a little put out that Hywel had taken control of the situation, but then, realising what it was that Hywel held in his hands, he composed his features and bowed deeply. 'Of course, brothers. Follow me now, and we will catch Father Abbot before he has his supper.'

Philip could have sworn he saw William glance back at the wine cask and lick his lips. Hywel winked at him as they fell in behind William, but kept his face straight. Philip's stomach was turning over, but not from hunger. The next few minutes, and how the abbot received him, would determine his future here. He sent up a quick prayer for calm, and readied himself.

The abbot had his own separate accommodation. On the same level as the monks' dormitory but accessed by a separate set of stairs, it ran the length of the south side of the cloister above the monks' refectory. They entered through a heavy wooden door into a window-lit long room, with a bed at one end. It was simply furnished but Philip noted touches of luxury: a pair of ornate gilded candlesticks, and a red velvet cushion or two. A large round table with six carved wooden chairs dominated the middle of the room. To one side under a tall window was a wide desk, piled high with manuscripts and writing implements. A few randomly placed wooden shelves held useful items and further books.

William had knocked but entered without waiting for a word of admission. He was obviously used to coming and going as he pleased. The abbot was standing by the window, seemingly more interested in what was going on outside than what was on his desk. He was a small man and stooped with age. He did not seem aware of their arrival.

'Father Abbot.' William stepped over and touched him on the elbow. The abbot turned and acknowledged the monk, and then saw his visitors.

'Brother Hywel.' Abbot Thomas approached him, bowing slightly, but kept his hands firmly clasped before him inside his wide sleeves. He turned then to Philip, who noticed that the old man's eyes were clouded with age, and that he was seemingly struggling to focus on the stranger in their midst.

William hurried over to stand between them. 'Brother Robert, from France. Another horse man. Joining us at Cymer, by your leave.' He spoke loudly and slowly, as if speaking to a child, and Philip bristled on the abbot's behalf.

The abbot nodded slightly, and then released his hands to shoo William aside. He stepped closer to Philip, examined his face closely, and seemed to make his mind up about what he saw there.

'There is always room for one more here, if you are prepared to *work*.' The voice was surprisingly strong for such a feeble man. 'You will see that I am no longer much use to the community here. I see less and less, and I hear very little. But this is a good place to see out one's days and I think you will be happy here.' He turned and nodded to William. 'He has my welcome, Brother Prior, see that he has yours,' he said, firmly.

'Father,' Hywel stepped forward, into the abbot's sight line. 'We brought you this gift. It is well travelled, but intact. The best wine Bordeaux could produce.' He spoke slowly and clearly, but without condescension.

'Ah,' the abbot allowed himself a small smile, as he saw what was in Hywel's hands. 'My thanks, brother. It is a long time since I had a fine wine to warm my old bones.' He nodded for William to take it. Philip was sure that he would not be drinking it alone if the prior had anything to do with it. 'And now I must eat. And you have my leave to join the lay brothers for supper yourselves tonight.'

He turned away from them then, to take his seat at the table. A monk appeared in the doorway bearing a tray with bread and fruit on it. Hywel took Philip's arm. They left the room and made their way down to the refectory to see what supper they could find for themselves.

It didn't take long for Philip to fall into the routine of daily life at Cymer. He was grateful for his preparatory time at Cwmhir, and the lessons learned with Hywel and Julian. He found he could adjust himself relatively easily to the Cistercian way of life.

Once his arrival had been accepted by the abbot, and seemingly tolerated by the prior, he found the other members of the community all welcoming in their own way. He had taken Hywel's advice and made himself available at every opportunity to work beside the brothers, turning his hand to a variety of tasks he had never done before, including milking the goats. He loved watching Brother Huw with the sheep, talking to them as if they were his children, and singing to them in his native tongue. He appreciated the honey that Brother David's bees produced, but was still wary to get too close to the hives, being happier to suffer David's teasing than be stung himself. David was also a gifted herbalist and the Abbey infirmarer, so always had a salve ready to treat the inevitable bee sting.

He found being in Meurig's company the most soothing. The older monk was happiest either bent over a spinning wheel or methodically carding fleece, or sat at his writing desk in the monks' day room. Philip was most fascinated by how steady a hand the monk still had, and how clear an eye, that he could produce the most intricate and beautifully coloured illuminations Philip had ever seen. He longed to try his hand at it, and got his opportunity one day when Meurig silently passed him a parchment that had been scraped back[8] for reuse, and a feather quill wet with ink. Before long, Philip discovered an aptitude for illustration that he didn't know he had, and the two sat happily alongside each other for hours, producing decorated manuscripts. All this on top of the time he spent working with Hywel in the stables.

The Rule of Silence was not easy for him, and Philip particularly missed his conversations with Hywel. They found time to talk sometimes while out in the field or yard with the horses, but there was often a lay brother within hearing distance, so it limited what they could talk openly about.

---

[8] This would be a *palimpsest* – a piece of used parchment taken from a book, that would have had the text scraped off. Parchment was expensive. Meurig would not have given him a new piece to try his fledgling skills on.

One day they found themselves alone in the field with just horses for company. It was a stifling hot, dry summer day and they had both independently taken the opportunity to take their midday rest hour in the cool of the shade provided by the trees that lined the field boundary.

Philip came across his friend, sitting with his back resting against a huge oak. His eyes were closed, but he opened them reluctantly when he heard Philip approaching.

'Hywel, am I disturbing your rest, brother?'

'No, my friend, sit with me, please. It's good to have the opportunity to talk, and I don't think we will be disturbed here today.' Hywel moved over to make space for Philip to sit beside him. 'You have been here some weeks now, how are you finding it?' Hywel asked him, although he had closed his eyes and rested his head back again.

'I feel quite at home here. I love the simple way of life, the routines, the peace. It is doing me much good. Why, have you concerns for me? Have I done something wrong?'

Hywel laughed. 'No, I hear only good reports. You have done well in making yourself useful to the brothers. Your willingness to serve has not gone unnoticed, nor your ready smile.'

'I find I enjoy serving others, and working alongside the brothers. I suppose that is what community is all about, what attracts people to this way of life, perhaps? That, and devoting your life to God, of course?'

'You can't actually separate the two, you know.' Hywel opened his eyes and turned his head to look at Philip. 'A life devoted to God must be more than just private prayer and contemplation. It must look like something to others. Our faith must work itself out in how we live towards one another. Living in community like this enables us to do that. To learn to serve one another, but also to learn how much we need each other.' Hywel paused, looking pointedly at Philip.

'Go on,' Philip encouraged him. He obviously had something to say that he thought Philip needed to hear.

'Many of us grow up believing we are self-sufficient and don't need other people. We learn to rely on ourselves and not to trust others, often through painful experiences. We may even begin to resent others interfering in our lives. Answer me this. If you hadn't been near death when I found you, would you have let me help you?'

'Honestly, the man I was then, no. I would have done everything conceivable to push you away. Including being rude and abusive, probably.' Philip was ashamed to admit it, but it was the truth.

'So, you were forced to accept my help only because you were helpless to do anything about it?'

'Yes, I suppose so. I was used to looking after myself, relying on myself, and I didn't trust people to get close to me in any way. It was a kind of self-protection, I think.'

'Answer me another question, then. Do you think David needs your help with the bees? Or Huw with the sheep and goats?'

Philip laughed. 'No. In fact, I think I am often more a hindrance than a help to either of them.'

'Yet they accept your help willingly. That is living in community. We serve one another and we also make room in our lives and work for others to serve us. It's learning that we cannot operate in isolation, and that people have been placed in our lives by God to enrich our lives, and to show us more about ourselves, and ultimately about Him.'

'Like I saw in Julian, and in Samson and Anwen?'

'Yes, and I am sure you have seen things you admire in others here too.'

'I love how Meurig can bring the beauty out of God's written word with his illuminations. He inspires me,' Philip said softly.

'That is a creativity drawn from the Creator Himself. God loves creating beauty, and is very good at it. Just look around you to see how well He does it.' Hywel paused again, and looked up at the azure sky through the dappled green shade of the mighty oak. Then he turned back to Philip. 'But it seems you have something of the same creative gift also. I have seen some of your work. It is good, my friend.'

Philip smiled. 'I don't know how good it really is, compared to Meurig's mastery, but I do love it. Every time I finish an illustration, I feel such a sense of completeness. Like I have found some purpose to my day. Like I have been able to offer something of some worth back to God, and to His people.'

'Creativity allows us to do that. It draws on His beauty and it produces things that glorify Him. A form of worship in itself, even, if done with the right motives.'

'I find on days when I am struggling with my thoughts, or with the confinement of the Abbey walls, if I can create with my pen, that somehow it gives me a focus and helps clear my mind.'

'That is a gift from God to you, then.'

'It is.' A surprise gift, Philip thought, and his heart was full at the thought of God's goodness to him.

'I get the same sense of purpose and focus from seeing a horse respond to my training techniques, or watching a foal being birthed.'

They sat and watched the horses grazing in silence for some moments. Philip spotted Noble ambling over towards a group of mares, flicking his mane and trying to look impressive.

'So, how is my horse responding to your training techniques, then?' he grinned.

'Pah!' A laugh exploded from Hywel in response. 'He's a lost cause. Does his own thing when he wants to, and in his own time. The embodiment of an independent spirit!'

Philip laughed along. 'At least you had more success with me! I'm happy to no longer be independently minded. I like needing people and being needed. Most of the time... Just now, though, I need to shut my eyes more than anything else.' He settled back and the two of them snoozed companionably.

The days and months sped by. The seasons changed and the routines with them. With shortened days, the Abbey adopted the winter schedule for the times of the prayer offices. There was less work time, and more time for private prayer and contemplation, more indoors than out. Philip found himself appreciating even this. He was becoming more familiar with the liturgies, which gave him great comfort. His singing was improving. At first he had imitated Hywel and mouthed the words of the plainsong chants, but as he grew more confident, he added his weak tenor to the other voices and was amazed at how beautiful a sound it made.

He was reading the Psalms mostly in his private study. He thought back to when he had read them in the early days of his recovery at Grand Selve, where it was the complaints of the psalmist that spoke most to him. Now as he read the Psalms, it was the cries of praise, the promises of hope and the testimonies to God's faithfulness that spoke most into his situation. He could meditate on these, and hear God's voice speaking into his spirit and soul. He loved the Gospels also, and these he found himself reading as he was illuminating them, his pen being put to one side as the story of his Saviour gripped his heart. The man Jesus came to life in the words, and made him yearn to live a life modelled on His.

The long winter with its cold nights eventually gave way to spring again and the Abbey sprang to life, with new chicks and lambs, and fish jumping in the river. Before he knew it, Philip had been at Cymer for a year. He was content in this life, for the most part. On the odd occasion he would feel the need to escape, and would steal away, saddle Noble and ride up into the hills, going as high as he could, until he could look down and see the valleys and fields below, and on a clear day even see the sea glistening in the far distance. He would stay as long as he dared, trying to remember what it felt to live free, outside the Abbey, but deep inside himself wondering if he *could* live free. It was a fear he didn't want to admit to. Would he lose this inner peace? Would he lose this new man he had become, if he dared to try to live as a normal man again?

Other times he would sit at the refectory table, silently eating his vegetables, and try to imagine the taste of Anwen's mutton stew on his tongue. Or else he would lie awake at night dreaming of biting into a juicy capon leg, or a roasted side of venison. But that was just food for the body, he reminded himself reluctantly, and here he was receiving food for the soul, and for his spirit. Philip had even seriously started to consider taking his vows. He wasn't sure how he could do that without exposing the deception that he and Hywel had contrived, but he wondered if this was the life that God had for him, the reason that he had been given a new start. He was so grateful to God for his ongoing healing; mind, body and soul. God deserved Philip's whole life in response, surely?

He broached the subject with Hywel when next they had opportunity to talk alone. Hywel listened thoughtfully, but said little, as Philip gave him his argument for staying on as a Cistercian.

'I cannot give you an answer to that particular question, brother,' Hywel responded eventually. 'I believe only God has the answer you are seeking. I only ask you not to hurry to make up your mind. Give it just a few months longer. Nothing need change here, on the outside, anyway. If you are not sure, then I believe you have your answer for now. *Are* you sure?' He looked intently at Philip.

Philip wasn't sure. Something niggled. 'I will take your wisdom as always, brother. I will take some more time to make my decision. Pray for me.'

'As I always do, as I always do,' Hywel smiled.

How sweet are Your words to my taste,

Sweeter than honey to my mouth!

Psalm 119:103, NKJV

Always give thanks to Father God for every person he

brings into your life

in the name of our Lord Jesus Christ. And out of your

reverence for Christ

be supportive of each other in love.

Ephesians 5:20-21, TPT

12
Efa

Early summer 1232

The slow-moving water of the River Mawddach glistened in the mid-morning sunlight. It was going to be a warm day, and it seemed as if all of God's creation was readying itself to celebrate it. The birds were singing and the wild flower heads were opening upward, worshipping the early summer sun, and perhaps in their own way, Philip mused, the One who had set the sun in the sky. Philip lifted up his own face and stood for a moment just revelling in the warmth and enjoying the peace, a once rare and lovely thing he now found so much easier to find, both externally and internally. Indeed, on days like this he could almost imagine having lived no other life.

In the distance he could hear the sound of Brother Aldred and the lay brothers splashing in the river shallows, pulling in the fishing lines and calling to one another, laughing among themselves, enjoying the warmth and joy the sun brought. Philip smiled to himself, and with a deep breath stirred himself out of his reverie. He had come to the river edge with a task to do, to find Brother Aldred and remind him that both he and the fish were required at the abbot's table sooner rather than later. He had been quick to volunteer to come, as the river always drew him. It had become a place where it was easy to rest and breathe deeply, a place for meditation and connection with God. Philip loved the quiet, cool spaces within the stone walls of the Abbey, and had learned to hear God in many of those holy spaces. But here, outside, among the trees, with his bare feet on the smooth round stones, lulled by the slow constancy of the wide river, and protected by the mountains rising in the distance; here, where creation was so alive with sounds and scents and colour; here was where Philip felt most alive to the Creator, where light and fresh air and cool water soothed his mind and soul and body.

Philip turned and started upriver towards the fishermen, but his attention was caught by a flash of light on steel in the far distance. A momentary surge of adrenaline put him immediately on guard, before he centred himself again in where he was and who he was now. As he focused on the area of forest above the river, he could pick out horses and the intermittent bright burst of colour from the riders' apparel, as they worked their way carefully down through the tall trees towards the wooden bridge that spanned the river where it narrowed close to the Abbey.

'The abbot's expected guests,' Philip said quietly to himself; even more reason for him to find Brother Aldred and his freshly caught fish. He didn't stop to watch the riding party continue their descent to the riverside; rather, he set out again to fulfil his commission. He knew it was Prince Llewellyn. He had been to Cymer many times before, to periodically inspect and select horses from the breeding stock Brother Hywel kept for him. His arrival always set the abbot and prior into a panic, and they would want the best of the garden's produce and the river's bounty to set before the prince and his retinue. The messenger this time had only arrived an hour before with the news that Llewellyn was calling in on his way back from Powys to his mountain retreat in Dolwyddelan. His purpose was to inspect the new foal sired by Noble that had already been noted for its potential. However brief his visit was going to be, the abbot would still want to make the best impression with the table he provided. The prince was the Abbey's most generous benefactor, after all.

As he made his way along the river edge, slipping his feet back into his sandals to negotiate the larger rocks, Philip heard the sound of the first horses' hooves hitting the bridge. Something made him stop. A sound he wasn't expecting – that of a high-pitched musical laugh, a woman's laugh – and not just any woman's laugh. A deep memory stirred within him and, closing his eyes for a moment, he saw himself back in the gardens at Swansea, running after Efa, chasing her and threatening her with all kinds of ridiculous torture for tricking him into eating a rotten apple, which to all intents and purposes had looked absolutely delicious. She had presented it to him polished and shiny, with the maggot hole well-hidden in her hand. Like her namesake, Eve, luring Adam with sin-laden fruit, Philip had looked into her smiling eyes and, being utterly beguiled, trusted her completely.

The sound of horses' hooves on wooden planks became deafening, and the laughter faded, but still he had to turn. Behind the men-at-arms and Llewellyn in all his splendour, rode two women. One was small and dark, riding with a stately air that marked her as nobility. The other was neither small nor dark. Her fair hair streamed down her back, and she sat more awkwardly on her mount; but it was she that drew him. Past and present collided in that moment, and Philip found his feet involuntarily walking towards the bridge, as if he had no control over any part of himself. Trancelike, he made his way towards her.

Something must have caught her attention, some sound or movement, and she glanced down towards him briefly, before turning back in the saddle and riding on. She must have seen him? But she showed no signs of having recognised him. But then, why would she? In his new guise, with his hair tonsured and in the white garb of a Cistercian monk?

Then, as if she were being drawn by his gaze, he watched as she slowed her mount, falling back from the group, and turned to look at him again. Close enough now so that their eyes met, for a moment everything around them stilled and disappeared. A look of confusion crossed her face, and then she shook her head, as if to free herself from a cobweb, and abruptly turned away, body sagging into the saddle as she kicked her horse forward to rejoin the group. Philip, still entranced, started as if to go after them, wanting the dream that could not be true to continue. He knew it wasn't really Efa, but he had to just pretend for a moment more that it was. Her lovely face, her glorious hair, her laughter.

He was rudely startled out of his dream by a slap on the back. He spun around and, out of habit, reached for the sword that was no longer there.

'Whoa! My apologies, soldier. Didn't mean to startle you. I'm no foe. Stand down, now!'

Philip refocused on the very real, solid form of the monk standing before him. Brother Aldred's round face was beaming, but his eyes were concerned.

'Forgive me, brother, old habits.' Philip, fully back in the present, smiled rather sheepishly at his brother monk.

'I presumed you were down here looking for me, chasing the abbot's fish. Well, come on, then, let's hasten back, and then you can get a closer look at those fair ladies that had you so mesmerised.'

'Oh, no, brother…' Philip began.

'No need to explain! We are still mortal men under these monks' habits. And the sight of a lovely lady is the pinnacle of God's creation, after all,' Aldred laughed. 'No harm in appreciating from a distance. It's not often we see such a beauty as the lovely Lady Joan among us poor sequestered men.'

Philip smiled to himself. Let him think it was the Lady Joan, with her raven hair, dark eyes and delicate pale complexion that had drawn his attention. As a king's daughter, and a prince's wife, she knew how to present herself in order to draw attention, and in her noble finery was indeed considered a beauty. But not as beautiful to him as the vision that the fair-haired lady had brought back into focus. His Efa had not been a celebrated beauty. She had been taller and broader than was thought ideal for a woman. Her hair was neither white-blonde nor russet brown, but somewhere in between, and when sun-bleached shone like spun gold, falling in loose waves around her face and shoulders. Her face, more often than not, was freckled and suntanned, and her features without distinction. But her blue eyes came alive with love and laughter, and shone out with a beauty that came from deep within her. Her smile was wide and her laugh infectious. She was fun and light and life, and so to him was beauty. In his dreams she was always laughing, or quietly smiling to herself as she concentrated on some task or other. He had only once seen her truly sad, truly heartbroken. But that heartbreak he had shared, and he would not allow himself to dwell in that memory.

By the time Philip and Aldred reached the Abbey, the horses were being led away to the stable block. Llewellyn and his retinue were being herded, rather like a flock of wild Welsh sheep, in through the narrow gateway that led to the cloister and the abbot's rooms beyond, by a nervously enthusiastic Prior William, all of a fluster at the appearance of not only the prince, but also his lady. The lady in question walked on the arm of her lord, and her fairer companion followed behind them, standing almost a head taller than Joan.

Philip could not help himself. 'Who is the lady with the Lady Joan?' he asked Aldred, trying to sound only vaguely interested.

'I'm not sure, my friend, as I have not seen her before. A waiting woman, I presume, although her fine dress rather marks her more as nobility. Perhaps she is a daughter of a Powys lord come to wed a Gwynedd princeling. You know how Llewellyn loves to arrange well-placed marriages to strengthen his hold on Wales.'

Philip's gut twisted momentarily. Yes, he knew all too well how Llewellyn's marital machinations could ruin lives.

He let Aldred wander off towards the kitchens with his basket of fresh fish, and turned towards the Abbey church. He was unsettled and agitated, and knew he needed some time alone and undisturbed. His memories had evoked a maelstrom of emotions, and he need to find his peace again. He made his way into the sanctuary, to a side chapel. The church was uninhabited, as the whole of the rest of the Abbey bustled around outside to accommodate their guests. It was cool and quiet inside the stone building, and sunlight shone through the high windows. He would pray and meditate a while, and refocus on the here and now and the life he had here, a life that contented him. He knelt and let his head fall, closing his eyes and breathing slowly and deeply. 'I need Your peace, God, come close to me,' he whispered in his soul.

Aware of only the sound of his own breathing and the feel of the warm sunshine as it kissed his shoulder, Philip stayed bowed and let God's peace flow over him. It was as if his soul breathed deeply, and found its way back to rest. Philip smiled to himself. It was so much easier these days, in this place, in this atmosphere, to recentre himself and let peace and joy quieten the tumult within. He thanked God for teaching him the simplicity of a devoted life, through the example and compassion of the true lovers of God who had become his teachers in this place. He was content – yet not content. But this was his life for now. The life he had chosen, or that had been chosen for him, and he chose to be content in that.

'Philip.'

His eyes shot open, but Philip remained frozen in position, his hands now tightly clasped together, and his breathing shallower. He dare not turn, dare not respond, dare not expose himself. It was Efa's voice. Just a whisper, but he would know it anywhere. It *was* her he had seen on that horse. How could she be here? He had long since relinquished any hope of ever seeing her again, and she had lived on only in his dreams and memories. It had been safer to keep her there, in a time where they could love and laugh and be together, before the cruelties of the world exposed them to pain and grief and separation. And now here she was in the flesh. Was she calling out to him? Did she know it was him?

'I am Brother Robert. You are mistaken. I am not who you think I am.' The words formed quickly in his mind, and he opened his mouth to speak them out loud but was silenced by the sound of a choked back sob.

'Father God, let me release my grief at his loss to You. Let me move on and find comfort for my heart. He is gone from this world, and with You now. I am grateful that he no longer suffers, but I suffer his loss, although I lost his love a lifetime ago.'

Philip tensed. She was talking to God, and not to him. It felt wrong to listen in to her private prayer. It was agony to hear her weep and to not respond, not run to her, soothe her, touch her. It was obvious to him now that she hadn't seen him where he knelt. He quietly shifted his position so that he could see around the stone column that hid him from her view. She was standing in front of the high altar, her face lifted up to the light streaming through the great windows, tears glistening on her cheeks. Her hands were clasped together in prayer but her back stood erect, as if she approached God as an honoured daughter and not some snivelling sinner. She spoke to God as if she knew Him intimately, pouring out her heart to Him like the psalmist of old.

She was never more beautiful to him, bathed as it were in heaven's light. Her clothes were good quality but not ostentatious; her hair was covered by a simple white veil but fell long down her back; she was more slender than he remembered and had lost her youthful bloom, but it was still Efa.

He must have made some sound, as she started and glanced around. Philip kept his head dipped and stayed where he was in the half-shadow of the column, feeling now like a naughty child hiding from his playmates, not wanting to be discovered but wanting to all at the same time.

'Forgive me for disturbing your prayers, brother, I did not see you there and thought I was alone.'

Philip composed himself before replying. 'Be at peace, my child.' Did that sound like a holy brother? He lowered the tone of his voice slightly. 'Don't let my presence disturb your own prayers, my lady. You seem to be carrying a heavy burden. I can withdraw and leave you alone, or perhaps help in some way?'

What was he thinking? What help could he offer her? Either as himself, or as a monk, he could not go to her in the way he wanted to. The most he could offer her was the comfort of a few well-meant words.

'Please don't leave on my account, brother. I had a shock, that is all. I saw someone and thought he was someone else. Someone I lost years ago. God knows my heart, and knows my grief. He has met me here and I can compose myself now. At least, I will be able to in a moment... My heart has learned not to carry the griefs and cares of this world, rather to leave them at the altar, and accept God's peace in place of them. I don't need to come to a physical altar to do that, but needed to escape the noise and company just for a moment. And I was drawn into this beautiful sanctuary.'

She spoke softly but with conviction. He watched as she turned back to the window and resolutely brushed the tears away from her face. He swallowed the emotion that tightened his throat. How much he wanted it to be his fingers brushing away those tears.

'Efa.'

What had brought her name to his lips? He shook himself. Perhaps she hadn't heard. But she had. She turned again. He rose to his feet, but still held back where she could not see him clearly.

'You know my name, brother?'

He knew then that he was lost to the inevitable. He could no more hide himself from her than he could hide himself from God. He stepped around the column and into the light. He willed his tongue to speak. 'I know your name, and I know your face, that form, those eyes, that voice. Efa, you were not mistaken when you saw me by the river.'

Philip stepped towards her and Efa stumbled backwards. He reached out a hand to grab her before she fell against the stone steps leading to the high altar.

'No... Philip?'

She sank down onto the steps, his hand still grasping her arm. 'But you are dead, killed in battle in France. I am grieving for you. I am breaking my heart over you – again. How can you be here? How can you be…' Her eyes looked him up and down in confusion, taking in his monk's guise, his leather sandals, his rough, undyed robe and his shaved head. 'A Cistercian? It doesn't make sense… I have to go.' She pulled her arm out of his grasp and staggered to her feet.

'Efa! Look at me. Truly.'

He reached for her and she let out a gasp as his hand touched hers. He saw her eyes close for an instant. There, the recognition, the memory of a touch; he felt it too. When she opened her eyes, they found his. He watched those beautiful eyes register the truth and come alive with realisation. For a moment everything stilled.

In the distance Philip thought he heard the sound of a bell clanging. Only it wasn't in the distance, it was right above their heads. The bell for Sext. The Abbey company would be descending on the church at any moment, dinner would follow, and then Llewellyn and his party would be leaving.

'Come quickly, with me.'

Philip spoke quietly but with urgency. She nodded ever so slightly, never taking her wondering eyes from his. He grasped her hand a little tighter, and quickly led her to the side door that led directly from the Abbey church to the fields beyond. Beyond the Abbey walls they stole through a field of uninterested sheep and into the forest. Philip led Efa to where a tree had fallen in the late winter storms, forming a natural place to sit, a hiding place of sorts.

'We cannot be long. I will most certainly have been already noted as missing from Sext, and you will soon be missed too.' Philip was breathing heavily, the urgency of the situation suddenly registering within him. 'There is so much we could say to each other, and we must talk quickly. But first, Efa, I must say sorry. Sorry for causing you pain, causing you grief, abandoning you…' He sat and pulled her gently down to sit beside him, the rough wood of the tree trunk solid beneath them.

'You had no choice leaving me the first time. I do not blame you for that. I knew I had lost you then, and I learned to live with that, on the surface anyway. We neither of us had any choice. We had our lives and our love stolen from us.' She did not face him as she spoke, and took her hand from his, placing it with her other hand demurely in her lap. She sat upright, more composed now, pulling away from him a little so that they did not touch.

'You married him!' Philip almost spat it out. 'I know you had no choice in marrying Cynan, but I could not bear it. And I could never forgive my brother John; he knew my hopes, how I felt about you, and yet the good opinion of his father-in-law, Llewellyn, was more important to him than his own brother's happiness. I could not stay to see you with another man, or live with the anger I felt towards John. I could have killed him! He laughed at my pain, calling me an immature boy and unacquainted with the politics of the real world we live in.'

She suddenly reached out to touch his cheek, as if to comfort the young man he had been, pulling her hand back quickly when she realised the intimacy of the touch. She bowed her head. Philip knew she was pulling on her own memories.

'I wept and railed at the injustice of it all, Philip. I wept for our lost hopes, I wept for our pain, and then I wept again when you left. But then I was done weeping and my heart grew hard. Life had to be lived, and I determined to make the best of it and not allow my heart to be hurt again. I married Cynan. He was not a bad man. It was not a bad life. It was just not the life we had dreamed of. Over time I even grew fond of him, but more like a daughter than a wife, he was so much older than I. He didn't want to add to his family and made no demands of me that might have led to more children. But I did have his to care for. My heart softened some in their company. I had to show them love, as they had no other mother to love them. And then God took hold of me, and my heart softened still more. I chose to forgive those who had wronged us. I chose to live free of bitterness. I chose a better way.'

'Was?' Philip had seized on that word. 'You spoke of your husband in the past tense.'

'I am a widow now, and alone. That is why I am with the Lady Joan. Llewellyn asked me to accompany them back north as Joan's waiting woman fell sick and had to be left behind. I agreed on one condition – that if I came into his household he would not force me to remarry. I would not be a pawn in his hands again.'

'And he agreed?' Philip was unconvinced.

'He did. His wife and his age have softened him, I think. He knows the difference now between a marriage of convenience and a true meeting of hearts. And I am quite determined. I will not be bartered for any price. My husband left me well provided for. I can live independently. Or perhaps I will find myself a place in a convent.' She lifted her head to look at him. 'It seems to me that you made that choice yourself?'

Philip sighed. 'Not exactly. It was chosen for me. I wanted to escape my life, and lying wounded in a French ditch, I longed for my life to end. Or for the strength to take my own life. But God had other plans for me, in the shape of Brother Hywel. He found me and tended to me, and brought me back here. We agreed for me to be disguised as a full brother. I did not want to be recognised, to be dragged back to a life I had despaired of. I had to have a new identity. Philip de Braose had to die in France.'

He saw a flicker of pain cross Eva's lovely face and her eyes grow wet. 'And so you did. News reached me some months ago that you were dead,' she continued softly, 'and all the grief of the past so carefully packed away in my heart came flooding back and, human that I am, I wept again for you.'

He took her hands in his and gently squeezed them.

'And then I saw you today, and I thought I had dreamed you into being. It was such a shock. I didn't know what to do, so I went to God. I thought perhaps I was hallucinating. That my grief had imagined your face onto that of another man.'

'It was the same for me, seeing you, or thinking that I had seen you, and yet not believing it could be you.' Philip squeezed her hands again, as if to convince himself she was real. 'So much of my old life, Efa, has been put to death. By my choice, and through the healing grace of God. And yet you, the memory of you, I could never erase, nor wanted to. You were the brightest, most alive part of my life. You were a dream I returned to again and again in my darkest moments. Even though I could not be with you, you never left me.'

They sat in silence for a moment, contemplating the enormity of what had passed between them, not looking at each other, but finding comfort in the simple touch of hand on hand.

'And so Philip de Braose is dead? And this is your life now?' She spoke first to break the silence.

'I wanted him dead, yes. But now... now, I don't know. I am content, I have learned so much, and have lived a different, better life here. But seeing you again... knowing that you are free...'

'We cannot go back to what we were.'

'No, and at this moment I cannot answer as to whether we can go forward,' Philip answered, honestly.

'Then it is enough that we have met again here.' It was said with resignation.

'It is more than I could have hoped for to see you, touch you, be near you again.' He reached up his hand to turn her face to his so that she could see the sincerity in his eyes. 'But I am not whole yet, Efa. I have been broken and have been mended, but I am not fully whole. Not just my body and its physical scars, but my heart, soul and spirit. Do you understand?'

He held her gaze until she smiled briefly and then bowed her head.

'More than you could know, Philip, I do understand. I will pray for you.'

Another pause. Then she breathed the inevitable.

'Will we see each other again?'

'I think that must be left in God's hands, Efa.' He thought again, trying to find her an acceptable answer. 'I cannot voice what it is I desire most in this moment. Or what God desires for me, for us both.' She looked up at him; he wanted her to see how much it pained him to admit to these truths.

'Then pray for me also, Philip, that our heart's desires and God's will be as one.'

The sound of the dinner bell rang out in the distance. Efa gently took hold of his hand as they walked back together, in a silent but strained harmony, one in soul and spirit, yet knowing they must part. Once in sight of the Abbey, Philip pulled on her hand to stop her for a brief moment.

'You will keep my secret?' he whispered, not daring to turn towards her, hoping he knew it was not distrust of her that made him speak.

'To expose it would cause potential pain to both of us. Your secret is safe with me.'

He glanced at her and she smiled at him, but the smile did not reach her eyes. Then with a quick squeeze of his hand she left him, walking purposefully back towards the opening in the Abbey wall. She stopped there for a moment, seemed to take a deep breath to fortify herself, turned, smiled again and lifted her hand. It was a sight that would imprint itself on his brain. She loved him still, he knew it, and he knew he would love her forever.

Pour out all your worries and stress upon him and

leave them there,

for he always tenderly cares for you.

1 Peter 5:7, TPT

Make God the utmost delight and pleasure of your

life,

and he will provide for you what you desire the most.

Give God the right to direct your life,

and as you trust him along the way

you'll find he pulled it off perfectly!

Psalm 37:4-5 TPT

13
Noble

Noble snickered a greeting as Philip slid quietly inside the stable, where the huge horse was contenting himself with the sack of oats that had been left open beside him. He didn't look up, knowing that Philip was no threat to him, or to his feed. Noble had been left alone in the stable, being the cantankerous old man that he was, the other horses having been turned out much earlier in the day to enjoy grazing in the summer sun. The horses of Llewellyn's party had joined them in the field, after being rubbed down and watered. Hywel had rightly decided it best not to chance Noble with strange horses. He seemed to prefer his own company these days, and apart from when called upon to service a mare, was happy to stay well away from the others. He had been known to kick out when bothered, and Hywel wouldn't have taken the chance of one of Llewellyn's fine horses being injured by the great brute.

The warm day made the stable stuffy, and the smell of horse flesh and soiled straw stung Philip's nostrils as he leaned in to rest his head and hand against Noble's neck.

'How are you, old boy? Is Hywel treating you well?'

Noble paused with his mouth full of oats, and made one great nod with his head, causing Philip to chuckle. 'As long as you are fed well and left alone to your own devices, eh?'

'Hywel is spoiling him rotten as always. And Hywel has been kept very busy today, no small thanks to you. Could have done with your help with the horses today, brother.' Brother Hywel sauntered into view, a wry smile on his face, his habit and scapular tucked up into his belt and a huge rake in his hand. Philip reached to take the rake from him and proceeded to muck out the stall next to Noble's.

'Sorry.' He gave no explanation. 'How did it go with Llewellyn? Was he suitably impressed with Seren's foal?'

'As we thought he would be. Yes, he sees his potential and wants him, as soon as he can be weaned from his mother. He even named him – Gwynt.'

'Wind? Yes, that suits him. He is going to be strong like his father here, and fast and light like his mother. Perfect fighting horse for these Welsh hills. Did he inspect the other horses? I was afraid he would covet Noble for himself.'

Hywel laughed in reply. 'Don't fret, your horse is safe here. He did come to the stable, but Noble bared his teeth and kicked out at him. I swear he makes himself unattractive. I hadn't managed to groom him today either, so he was looking a bit worse for wear; showing his age, you might say.'

Noble snorted loudly in the next stall.

'He's a good judge of character, that horse, and as temperamental as any old seasoned soldier. I would have bared my teeth at Llewellyn too if he had approached me!' Philip admitted, wryly.

Hywel laughed again. 'Probably just as well you were out of the way, then.' He stood, hands on hips, and looked pointedly at Philip.

Philip knew Hywel deserved an explanation as to his absence, but he wasn't in a hurry to give it. Hywel was a patient man; he knew he would wait. Philip applied himself again to the task of raking out the soiled straw.

'Here, I'll do that. You see if Noble will let you take a brush to his filthy back.'

Hywel handed him the brush and took the rake from his hands.

'He trusts you,' he said, nodding at the horse.

'And I him. We go back a long way,' Philip replied. 'I'm glad Llewellyn didn't want him. I couldn't bear to be parted from him…

'I have lost too much already today,' he added under his breath, gulping down the wave of emotion that suddenly threatened to spill out of him. He concentrated on the task at hand. Efa had gone, and it was right that she went. And he would pray, and maybe God would permit that they might see each other again. Perhaps she wasn't completely lost to him? But seeing her so unexpectedly, and then parting from her again – that had left him in some turmoil.

He had gone back to the shade of the trees after she had walked out of his sight, unwilling to be in company, even the silent company of the refectory. He hadn't wanted to see her leave the Abbey, for fear that he might have chased after her, hung on to her somehow, embarrassed them both. He had waited until he was sure that the horse party had left and then made his way quickly and quietly to the stable block and out of the way of prying eyes. He knew his absence at Sext and at the meal table would have been noted, and Prior William would be on the warpath.

'This horse saved my life.' He focused on the sure, solid form of Noble, brushing his broad, dark neck and following each brush stroke with an affectionate stroke of his hand.

'Yes, I believe he did. I wouldn't have found you if I hadn't stopped to see why such a fine hulk of horseflesh had been left abandoned on the side of the road, with his saddle and tack still intact. He was standing by you, and must have been for the whole day and night you lay in that stinking ditch. He was agitated as I approached. He would not let me lead him away, rather pulled me towards the ditch. Then I heard a groan, and looked down, and there you were. And there our strange acquaintance began.'

'I am forever grateful to the both of you. To you, for all you did then, and for all you have done since.' Philip smiled briefly at the monk. 'And Noble here deserves all the spoiling he can get. He fought well, and was my constant reliable and trustworthy companion for many years. He saw many of the awful things I did, and I'm sure carries his own scars.' Philip leaned into Noble and whispered in his ear. 'We are safe here, boy.'

They carried on working in silence for some time, before Hywel spoke again.

'She is a fine lady, that Lady Efa.' Hywel didn't pause in his work. It wasn't a question, just a statement, a cracked-open door maybe.

Philip allowed himself another small smile. So Hywel had noticed more than he had given him credit for. He knew he had that ability, whether by observational skills or a sixth sense. Philip didn't answer, but waited, continuing to methodically groom Noble, knowing there would likely be more to come from Hywel.

'She must have gone for a walk, as she came in flustered and late for the abbot's table.' Hywel looked pointedly at Philip.

'Were you not in the refectory for dinner, brother?' Philip replied, just as pointedly.

'I was invited to join the meal at the abbot's table, as Llewellyn wanted to continue talking horses, and the Rule of Silence is not so strictly adhered to with such prominent guests at table,' Hywel explained. 'The Lady Efa was only a little late, made her rightful obeisance to both the abbot and the prince, and quickly and quietly sat down at the table to eat. Although I don't think she ate much, from what I saw.'

Philip sighed, letting his hands drop. Noble shook his head, neighing softly, unhappy that the brushing and stroking had stopped so abruptly.

Philip took a deep breath. 'You know I will tell you all, don't you?' He glanced over to where Hywel stood patiently, leaning on his rake.

'There is no one here but you me and that old horse, brother. You can speak openly, but only if you want to. It may help to unburden yourself.'

'You know me well enough to know that it will.' Philip sighed again. 'Efa was – she is – the finest of ladies. To me, anyway.'

'You knew her.'

'Knew her and loved her… love her.'

The truth exploded from his lips, with all the pent-up emotion of the last few hours, like a taut bowstring releasing an arrow to flight.

Hywel gave him a moment and then spoke again, softly, 'Then she was the reason for your heartbreak as a young man?'

'The object of my great betrayal, yes.' The brush slipped from Philip's hands, which now formed tight fists hanging down by his sides. He leaned his head onto Noble's broad back, and the horse never shifted, as if he were sensing the support Philip needed.

'Come, sit, Philip.'

This too was said softly, Philip noticing that Hywel dared to use his real name, apparently sensing it was right for the moment. Hywel leaned his rake against the stable wall, wiped his sweaty brow with his broad sleeve and then pointed over to a fresh pile of straw in the corner, under a window opening in the wall that allowed a cooling breeze into the stable. As they moved to sit down, Noble, instinctively, it seemed, moved himself so that his body made a barrier between them and the open door of the stable, hiding them from prying eyes. The horse helped himself to a generous mouthful of fresh hay that was hanging in a bundle from a hook on the wall, and stood chewing, with his ears up, as if also readying himself to hear what Philip was about to say. Philip sat down with Hywel to his left, with enough space between them so that he could see the monk's face half-turned towards him.

'You know some of the history of the de Braose family?' Philip began, and Hywel nodded.

'You may know, then, of my grandfather William and the atrocities attached to his fame? How my grandfather fell out with the late King John, and how his wife, Maud, my grandmother, and his eldest son, my own father, William, were imprisoned and left to die in Corfe Castle?'

Hywel nodded again.

'I was but a young boy, not yet ten years of age, when they died. My grandfather had already fled to France, and my mother abandoned us and died herself not long after. I was left with my brother John in the care of my uncle, Giles, Bishop of Hereford. We lived in various places, but predominantly here in Wales on the Gower, far enough away that hopefully the king would forget about us. I have only vague memories of that time; it never felt safe and we never stayed long in one place. The only constant in that time, apart from my brother, was a priest, a trusted friend of my uncle Giles, entrusted with our care and education. Gerallt was his name. A gentle soul. Grey-haired and frail, but strong in heart and mind and faith. He, I suppose, was the reason I have never been able to fully escape God.' Philip glanced at Hywel. 'It was Gerallt who introduced me to God as Father, you see, when I had no earthly father left. I saw in Gerallt what I have seen here. That it is possible to have a relationship with God that goes beyond religious observance, rituals and sacraments.'

He paused. Recalling Gerallt at least made him smile. He braced himself to speak again. These were not easy memories to retell.

'We were not safe. King John remembered us, and when I was but fourteen years old, and my brother sixteen, he tracked us down. I suppose he thought we were old enough to be a threat to him, and he feared the de Braose name, perhaps understandably, knowing the ruthless man my grandfather had been. We spent the next four years in his custody. Berkeley was our prison, although it was not all bad. Robert de Berkeley was not the greatest supporter of King John, and only took us in to keep himself in favour. We were well cared for, if confined within the castle walls. He even let us train with his squires, which is how I learned to handle a weapon, and I grew in physical strength as I grew into manhood. My great regret at that time was losing Gerallt. But I had my brother, and we had grown very close, and dependent on one another.

'And then, King John died, and young Henry came to the throne, and everything changed again. My brother John was granted my late father's lands, and we were released from our captivity. A year later my brother made a brilliant match, marrying Marared ferch[9] Llewellyn.'

'Llewellyn's eldest daughter by his mistress?' Hywel questioned.

'Daughter of Tangwystyl, yes, although as you probably know, a mistress is given different rights under Welsh law, and her offspring regarded as legitimate, so it was considered a good match for a young Marcher lord.[10] Anyway, Marared came with a sizeable dowry – the Lordship of Gower. Llewellyn was shrewd; he too feared the de Braose name, especially once we were seemingly back in favour with the crown. He likes to keep his potential enemies close by, and giving Gower to my brother kept him as an ally.

'With Marared came her cousin as her waiting woman. Efa was fifteen when she came to Swansea. She was the orphaned daughter of Tangwystyl's brother, and Llewellyn's ward. I was eighteen. Barely a man, and yet enough of a man to appreciate the company of an attractive young woman. She was full of life and light and joy, and after the darkness of my early years I was drawn to her as a moth to a flame. We laughed and talked, and got up to mischief together, all the while realising that we were forming the deepest of attachments. We saw no barrier to our romance. We believed John and Marared would both look kindly on us being wed. We were sorely mistaken, however.'

Philip shifted his position a bit, and Noble bowed his head to nudge him for a stroke. He smiled up into the horse's eyes.

---

[9] 'Ferch' is Welsh for 'daughter of'.

[10] The Gower was a Marcher Lordship, lands usually given to Norman nobles by the English King, but in this case held by Llewellyn. Marrying the Welsh prince's daughter was a good political move for John de Braose and helped secure his Welsh lands.

The horse was finely attuned to his mood; it was as if he was giving him the courage to continue baring his soul. His other confessor sat quietly, seemingly mesmerised by the stalk of straw he was twirling in his hands. He looked up when Philip paused. 'Your brother stood in the way of the match?'

Philip absent-mindedly stroked the horse's muzzle. He sighed as he continued.

'Llewellyn came to Swansea, and with him he brought some of the household of the princes of Deheubarth; among them a new friend, Cynan ap Cynan. He was an older man and a widower, looking for a wife to be a mother to his three young children. He saw Efa, and decided that she was the girl he wanted. And she was barely seventeen at that time. Llewellyn was well known for using marriages to his own political advantage, and so with little thought for Efa's feelings, or those of anyone else, he agreed that Cynan could have her. In his mind, I suppose, he thought he had done well in providing a good match for his orphaned ward. Efa was little more than a pawn in his political game. She begged him to let her stay in Gower, to let her marry me. I, on the other hand, begged my brother to plead our case with Llewellyn. He refused. He did not want to cross the great man, and for Marared's sake and to hold on to his own power, he decided it wiser to agree wholeheartedly to the match. He even threw a celebration meal to honour Cynan and Efa's betrothal. He ridiculed me openly during that meal, when he was drunk, laughing at me as *the boy* who thought he could marry for love.'

Philip was clenching his fists again, and Noble wisely stepped away to give the barely suppressed anger space.

'And so you thought he had betrayed you?' The question was gentle.

'He *had* betrayed me! I thought I meant more to him than that. I thought he would fight for my happiness – for *our* happiness!'

Philip tried hard to contain the rage that had boiled up from deep within him; a rage that Efa's appearance had brought flooding back. He had thought that all the anger in him had been long dealt with.

'He may have felt he had no choice himself, Philip.' Hywel continued to speak gently, but firmly.

Philip paused at that. 'We always have choices,' he ground out.

Hywel was sat with his elbows on his knees, contemplating the tiny pieces of dust that swirled in the sunlight coming through the window opening above. The ensuing silence lingered between them.

Philip used the quiet to bring his emotions under control, a technique perfected during his fighting years. He regulated his breathing, sat up, spine straight, and stretched his neck, back and shoulders. A pretence at control.

A loud grumbling interrupted the peace.

'Ha,' Hywel laughed quietly. 'So you do regret missing dinner, then? Just as well Brother Aldred whispered to me to let you know there would be a plate for you hidden behind the kitchen door, if you didn't leave it too long. You just need to get to it before William gets to you!'

Philip rubbed his stomach subconsciously and stood up with the help of Noble's mane. He led the horse back into his stall. 'Where would I be without good and constant friends?' he said, as he rubbed the horse's ears. Glancing back he smiled thoughtfully at Hywel. 'Thank you, too, for your friendship, Hywel.'

'Thank God, my friend. There is none more faithful than Him. You have experienced broken friendships, and you have had enduring ones.' Hywel nodded towards the horse. 'But there is One who has never left your side. God will never betray you. You can trust *Him* always, believe me.'

A man who has friends must himself be friendly,

But there is a friend who sticks closer than a brother.

Proverbs 18:24, NKJV

14
Hywel

Clang. Steel against steel. Philip roared with rage as he met each stroke of his brother's sword with his own. He was younger than John, and had more years of war-won strength, and fighting ability. His brother had grown plump and slow with his years of domesticity, and although bigger than him, was no match for Philip. Now he would have his revenge! All the years of pent-up anger and hurt ploughed into his sword arm as he struck, and struck again. Bit by bit, he was edging John backwards towards the keep wall, and he would have him then, cornered like the frightened rabbit he was. John's eyes grew wide with terror as he felt the solid stone behind him – he knew he was trapped. Philip swung his sword around and used the hilt to smash against John's wrist, causing him yelp in pain and drop his sword. With his other hand, Philip grabbed John around the throat.

'Now I have you, betrayer!' he spat into his face.

John's terrified eyes glanced over Philip's shoulder.

'You'll get no help from him,' Philip sneered. Behind them lay the great hulking figure of Llewellyn, gurgling in his own blood, with Philip's dagger sticking out from his neck. 'He is soon dead, and you will soon follow!' Philip raised his sword to strike.

Clang. Clang. What was that? More swords? Whose swords? They were alone, Philip was sure. He held his sword aloft and his grip tightened on John's throat, poised to strike but suddenly hesitant.

Clang. Clang. No, not swords… a bell clanging. Loud, and getting louder. A bell? Philip shook his head in confusion.

And then suddenly he was awake. His eyes flew open, the sweat pouring off him. He sat up in bed, his breath coming in deep gulps. He looked down at his wet hands, expecting to see blood, but there was none. They were wet from perspiration and he was trembling all over. He swung his legs around, grounding his feet on the cool wooden floor, and put his hands over his ears. The clanging of the bell was chiming in time with the thumping in his head.

'Philip?'

He started, and looked up to see a shadowy figure in white looming above him.

'It's me, Hywel,' the figure whispered. 'The bell is sounding for Vigils. I heard you shout out as I was passing your cell. A bad dream?'

Philip shook his head slowly from side to side, trying to clear it. At least the clanging outside his head had ceased. He looked around and in the moonlight could see the comforting walls of his cell, his simple bed with its dishevelled covers, the table. He wasn't in Swansea, he wasn't sword fighting, he hadn't killed…

Philip groaned in anguish. 'I killed them. I was killing them…'

'Who?'

'Prince Llewellyn, and John, my brother. It was so real, the emotions… I wanted them dead… I wanted to kill them.' He dropped his face into his hands, shaking with emotion.

'Come, brother, it was just a dream.' Hywel talked softly, but urgently. 'We will talk later, I promise you. We must go now. You must at least make an appearance at Vigils or Prior William will most definitely seek your excommunication, missing a second office in two days without good excuse.'

Trying to coax Philip back into the real world, Hywel helped him to his feet, and handed him his belt. He held on to him as

Philip shakily fed his feet into his sandals, and then, sure he was awake and upright enough to walk by himself, Hywel led the way down the stairs, through the cloister and into the church. It was impossible to know if anyone else had heard Philip cry out, or if they noticed his slightly disarrayed state, but they joined their brothers with a modicum of decorum at least. Philip dropped into the seat next to Hywel. He let the now familiar words of the liturgy wash over him, and then as the pure, clear singing voice of Brother Pedr led the chants, he finally began to feel peace descending on his troubled soul.

Leaving the church and heading into the cloister after prayers, Hywel walked alongside Philip, their hands tucked into their sleeves across the front of their bodies, to ward off the early morning chill. They had time now for silent contemplation before Lauds, and then would return to the church for Prime at sunrise. Philip and Hywel wouldn't be able to get to the horses until at least 5am, when the monks were released to work. They were supposed to stay silent until then, but it was possible to whisper without turning your head, and to hope that your companion was tuned in enough to pick up your words.

'I'll be mending fences at the far side of the horse paddock, closest to the river. I could do with your help today,' Hywel whispered into the air.

Philip smiled to himself and nodded his head ever so slightly. Inside he laughed. They had mended those fences not more than a week ago. Still, that would take them far enough away from the Abbey to be able to talk undisturbed, and maybe find their way to the peace of the riverbank too.

The sun was already high in the sky as Philip made his way across the dew-wet grass of the horse paddock. All of the horses, except troublesome Noble, were already out and grazing. Philip had been waylaid by William, and had offered a weak excuse for missing Sext the day before, mumbling something about losing a sandal in the woods. He had to then endure the expected lecture from the pompous little man, who had set himself up as the overseer of their souls – in his own mind, at least. Philip bore the tirade about the seriousness of the vows they had taken, without releasing the smile that threatened to expose him. If only William knew that he had broken no vows, because he had never made any! But William did not need to know his story, or who he really was. So, by the time Philip had escaped William's tongue-lashing, Hywel had already let the horses into the field, and was where he said he would be at the far end of the paddock, leaning casually on a very solid, recently repaired fence.

'Well, shall we walk, brother?' Hywel said, smiling at Philip as he approached. 'I have a story of my own to tell you today.'

They ducked through the fence and into the trees that lined the riverbank. Once clear of the trees, they negotiated some rocks, until they found a spot where they could sit, close to the river's edge. The newly risen sun was beginning to warm the stones, and the river was sparkling in the morning light. They would be undisturbed here, except by the kingfisher swooping in and diving for his early morning fish. The fishermen were not out; it would be back to grains and freshly produced garden vegetables for the monks today.

Not until they were sat with their backs against rocks and their legs outstretched towards the water did Hywel speak.

'I knew a young man once. Not unlike you, not so long ago, I suppose,' he began. 'He was the second son of a land-wealthy Norman nobleman; his father not quite a de Braose but powerful enough in his own right. This young man was destined for the Church, and had accepted his fate, but as the time grew near for him to leave his family home, he grew restless. He made the reasonable decision, in his own mind, at least, to experience the things of the flesh that he would soon enough have to deny himself. He was a personable young man, and not bad-looking. He was also an impressive horseman and attracted plenty of female attention. He was not cruel, nor unkind, and quickly found many a young lady who would willingly enjoy his company for a night or two, especially as he had coin in his purse, and would be generous with it.'

'You have me intrigued. Is this a romance? Or just a good old-fashioned bawdy tale? Long time since I heard one of those.' Philip winked at Hywel.

But Hywel had grown serious, his usually quick-to-laugh face pensive. 'Not quite, my friend. The young man was enjoying his freedom and his liaisons but still was not satisfied. There was one woman that he wanted more than any other, but there was a problem. She was already wed to another man. And not any other man, to a man who had been a long-time friend and confidant. A friend who had taught the young man all he knew about how to train, ride and care for horses, and how to breed them successfully. An older man, but a man to whom he had become deeply attached. His wife was young and beautiful. She was small and fine-featured, with hair red as autumn leaves and eyes of ethereal green. The young man was entranced by her. He had not lusted after her at first, seeing her only as the devoted wife of his good friend. But once he had tasted of the things of the flesh, he began to see her as men are tempted to see a beautiful woman, and he began to desire her. She was not immune to his charms either; he did not need to force himself on her. They only had to wait for an opportunity, and when it arose he gave in to his passion, and she to hers.'

'It was you, wasn't it? The young man was you?'

Hywel didn't answer. He continued his tale, all the time rubbing a small, round pebble in his hand. 'Cenred had been called away to a horse in foal on a farm more than half a day's ride away. He was known for his skills for many miles around and willingly responded when called on. Hild, his wife, and I, his friend, betrayed his trust. It was only once. Guilt drove us apart after that. I found my solace elsewhere, behaving all the more wildly in an attempt to erase her from my mind and heart, where she had found a lodging place. That liaison between us, however, led to a child, and that child led to Hild's death.' Hywel paused. He took the pebble and threw it into the shallows at the edge of the river.

'Ripples,' he said. 'Consequences. Every wrong decision, every wrong act, bears its own consequences.'

He sat in silence for a few moments, as they watched the ripples spread outwards from where the still water had been disturbed. Hywel began to speak again, his voice so quiet, Philip had to strain to hear him.

'I did not have to fear any other punishment for my sin, Philip. My grief and heartbreak were as real as Cenred's when Hild died. I grieved for his grief, I grieved for her loss, I grieved for the pain my recklessness had caused, and I grieved for the man it had exposed me to be. My guilt ate away at me, destroying me from the inside out. I was in despair. I could not bear being close to the man whom I had betrayed so badly, and to the places that evoked the memory of what I had done, and so I resolved to enter the Church as soon as it could be arranged. Another running away, I suppose.'

Hywel looked pointedly at Philip for a moment.

'But God had other plans for me. He had one more lesson to teach me before I vowed to serve Him for the rest of my life. Seemingly Hild had confessed all to Cenred when she found herself with child, as they had never consummated their marriage. He never rejected her, or punished her in any way for betraying him, choosing instead to pledge to raise her child as his own, to keep them both under his protection, and to keep our secret. He never once said anything to me, never confronted me, or changed in his behaviour towards me. He let me comfort him in his grief, and held my hand to comfort me in mine as they buried her.

'Not many weeks later, Cenred himself lay dying. Some said it was of a broken heart, but he had picked up a fever during a cold, wet night saving a horse stuck in a flooded ditch. He asked for me to come to him, and I went, not knowing what I would say. Should I absolve myself, or let him die believing me his true friend? It was then I realised that he knew the truth already. He

183

grabbed my hand and drew me close to him, and almost with his last breath, he absolved me. He forgave me, Philip!' Hywel's voice broke slightly. 'He was a far, far better man than me.

'He still loved me deeply, and he saw that my guilt would destroy my life if I didn't deal with it. "I forgive you," he said. "Now you must learn to forgive yourself." It didn't take me long to realise that in what Cenred had done for me was a living example of how God forgives, Philip. He loves us so much that He is willing to forgive us over and over again. He gave us His Son so that we can live guilt-free. We confess our sins and He forgives us, absolves us freely. I learned too that forgiveness, forgiving others, is one of the most powerful keys we have to unlock chains of guilt, offence and anger in our own lives.'

Hywel stood and walked to the water's edge. Philip scrambled to join him.

'If I were to throw a hook and line into this river and catch a fish,' said Hywel, 'when I landed it, I would take the hook out of its mouth. When we forgive someone who has hurt us, it is not letting them off the hook, or in any way minimising the wrong they have caused us, because they will have to face both the consequences of sin and the judgement of God for their wrong actions if they do not repent. Forgiving someone is actually taking the hook out of our own mouth – or out of our own heart, perhaps. If left in place, that hook can fester, leading to offence, bitterness, hatred, anger and revenge, leading us into making more wrong decisions, causing more hurt.'

He turned towards Philip and placed his hand on his arm. 'Deep down, you know that you have not forgiven John, and you haven't forgiven Llewellyn. That was evident as you told me your story yesterday. Just because it happened many years ago, and you have buried the feelings well, doesn't mean that the wound is healed. I can tell you, from my own experience, that forgiveness is the key... to your freedom, your healing, for you to move on. I assure you, you will feel a lighter man when you can find it in your heart to forgive. And I believe once you have forgiven them, you will sleep a dreamless sleep again.'

'You make it sound so easy.' Philip looked intently at Hywel, wanting to believe it *was* possible to find that freedom Hywel spoke of.

'It isn't easy. Everything within us fights against it, especially when those who have hurt us never ask for our forgiveness. Forgiving others is hard, but it is a choice God asks us to make – 'seventy times seven',[11] Jesus told Peter, when he asked how many times he must forgive his brother. And the Gospel story reminds us over and over how much more God has forgiven us. If He can forgive us for all that we have done in disobedience to Him, how much more should we be willing to walk in that forgiveness by forgiving others? Think on it, Philip; that is all I ask. And ask God for His help to make the right choice.'

Hywel turned and started back across the stones and towards the tree-lined bank, and to the horses that would soon need his attention. Philip followed him, deep in thought.

'The child – what happened to the child?' The question came unbidden to his lips and Philip berated himself when he saw Hywel's reaction. The monk stopped, dead still, and was standing with his head bowed. After a moment, Philip watched him lift his face to heaven and the light of the sun.

'My son…' His voice broke again. 'My son died in the arms of his dying mother.' He steadied himself and then turned to face Philip.

'My greatest pain, and my greatest guilt, was that not only had I caused his birth, but I had also caused his death. An innocent life. If you think forgiving others is hard, Philip, it does not compare with the struggle to forgive ourselves. Long after I knew both Cenred and God had forgiven me, I could not forgive myself. But in time, and in God's good hands, I have come to a place of peace with what I did. I still carry the pain, but it is tempered with joy now. I will see my son again, and I will hold him in my arms, and enjoy his presence forever in the presence of God.' He smiled then. 'Come now, we must get

---

[11] Matthew 18:22, NKJV.

back before we are missed. You are in trouble enough! And those horses need exercising, and I am not doing it alone today.'

Philip clambered up the bank behind Hywel, following him through the trees and back into the paddock. Some good hard physical work was just what he needed right now. He had much to think about.

Lay aside bitter words, temper tantrums, revenge,

profanity, and insults.

But instead be kind and affectionate toward one

another.

Has God graciously forgiven you?

Then graciously forgive one another in the depths of

Christ's love.

Ephesians 4:31-32, TPT

15
A Letter

Late autumn 1232

Philip followed Hywel into the warming room after Vigils. It was a cold morning and a long wait until the next office of Lauds, now that the approaching winter had shortened the days and sunrise was so much later. The time of contemplation between the two offices, for the older monks at least, meant huddling together in the warming room and closing their eyes to meditate. Heavy breathing often followed, with the odd gentle snore. Philip smiled to himself. He wasn't old enough to warrant being here, really, although his leg ached abominably on damp mornings like this. Outside the wind blew the rain sideways; 'proper Welsh rain', Hywel called it. Philip told himself he would only stay in the warming room long enough to warm his feet through and get some feeling back into his leg muscles, and then he would go and join the ascetically faithful in the cloister.

Philip sighed as he sat on the stone bench, stretching his legs out and rubbing his aching knee. Beside him, Aldred shifted, snored softly and slumped a little towards him. Philip gently prodded him upright without waking the plump monk. The long summer days out in the fields or down on the riverbank had passed blissfully by and now they were in the throes of autumn. The leaves on the great oak trees had turned from green to brown, and they had dropped their acorns for the scurrying squirrels to collect. The river was full, flowing fast with the mountain rain wash, and the grain fields had long since been harvested.

Philip took the quiet moment to contemplate the last few months at the Abbey. Like the changing of the trees, the river and the fields with the changing of the seasons, so he had been changed. Less visibly, perhaps, except to those who knew him best, like Hywel, and increasingly Aldred. The cellarer knew nothing of his secret life, and accepted him as the monk he portrayed himself to be, but was an old soldier himself and had recognised familiar traits in Philip. He too had made the journey from nightmares to rest, from conflict to peace. A stool in his warm kitchen had become a favourite escape spot of Philip's. He would sit and talk, recalling battle stories, or sharing things that God had revealed to him, and Aldred would hand him a bucket of beans to pod, or carrots to scrub, to make him appear useful.

He still worked most days with Hywel and the horses. There was always plenty to do. Noble was still his old cantankerous self, preferring Philip to tend to him rather than anyone else. He had deigned to get two more mares in foal over the summer, and the horse stock was looking promising. Hywel was contemplating another trip to France, if it could be arranged in the spring, to acquire more horses to breed from. Hywel certainly had grand plans, but Philip questioned whether the size of the Abbey and its enclosures would really support a much bigger operation. Still, men would always need good horses, and the Abbey did well financially out of Hywel's hard work and knowhow.

Philip's contemplation was disturbed by the sound of hooves approaching the Abbey, and the commotion as the porter rushed from the contemplation of his own eyelids to see who called at this time of the day. Night-time visitors were rare, but in weather like this... Philip shivered at the thought of being cold and rain-soaked on the back of a steaming horse. He wouldn't mind never being in that position ever again. He rose to his feet and Aldred grunted and slumped the opposite way. Brother Hywel looked up at him from across the room and his face held a question.

'I'll go,' Philip mouthed to him, and raised his hand palm-up to indicate Hywel to stay in the warm. The messenger's horse would need seeing to, and Philip would save Hywel getting chilled by taking care of it himself. He smiled down at the dozing form of Aldred; he'd save him from being disturbed too, by ensuring the visitor had a warm drink and a seat by the kitchen fire. The lay brothers would have laid the fire already; that would aid him.

Philip stayed under cover as much as possible, hurrying around the cloister. One or two of the monks at prayer nodded as he passed. Brother William assiduously kept his focus on the dimly lit manuscript in front of him, and sniffed at the noise Philip made, as if it were he disturbing them and not the sound of a horse snorting and puffing, the rider dismounting with a thud outside, and the porter fighting with the wind to keep the door open. Pulling his hood up, Philip ran outside to greet the visitor.

'Come,' he said, taking in the bedraggled young man with his dark hair plastered wet to his head, and his clothes dripping. 'You and that poor horse need to get dry.'

He took hold of the horse's reins and, nodding to the visitor to follow, led them around to the relative shelter of the stables. The other horses shuffled and neighed at the intrusion, and Noble lifted his great head once in greeting and then dropped it again, flicking his ears forward and half-raising one leg, preferring to sleep a bit longer than be bothered by the newcomer.

'I'll see to your horse. I'll tie him here, and come back to rub him down. I'll show you to the kitchens, first. You look dead on your feet.'

The young man had slumped against the wall, eyes glazed. Too exhausted to say much, he pointed at the saddlebag.

'Missive,' he said, 'from Prince Llewellyn. Important.'

Philip expected a tightening of the gut at the mention of Llewellyn's name. He waited for a second but none came. Interesting, he thought to himself. Maybe Hywel had been right about the power of forgiveness. He removed the sopping saddlebag, and grabbed the young man by the arm, preventing him from slumping even further down the wall. 'Come on, young man, with me.'

Hauling him to his unsteady feet Philip half-led, half-dragged him over to the kitchen. He was right about the lay brothers, the fire was already in and glowing. He just needed to stoke it a bit, adding some fresh wood, and it blazed invitingly. He sat the youngster on some sacking on the floor by the hearthside, not trusting him to stay seated upright on a stool. Quickly he warmed some honeyed ale in a pan over the fire and handed it to his guest.

'Take your wet things off; you won't be disturbed for a few hours in here. You can cover yourself with this,' he handed him a cloak that someone had conveniently left hanging on a hook behind the door, 'and get yourself warm. I think you best sleep a while before trying to explain why you are here, and why you arrived at this hour.'

'Got lost... first time. Thought I knew my way. Llewellyn... trusted me... I failed.' The boy shivered, desperately trying to force his words into a coherent sentence.

'Well, you haven't failed, because you are here now. Either your horse or God's provident hand got you to our door. Nothing is so urgent that it can't wait a few hours. You get yourself dry and as comfortable as you can, and I'll go tend to your poor horse.'

Philip squeezed the shoulder of the already half-asleep lad. He didn't think it likely that the messenger would do more than kick his wet boots off and remove his cloak before sleep would overcome him. He was fifteen or sixteen, maybe. Young to be out alone in these wilds. He was curious as to what message was so important to send him out in this weather, but he refused to badger the boy, and it would not be his concern anyway. They would get more from him when he had rested and was warmed. Prior William would be all fastidious and meddling, and have the messenger talking soon enough. He hung the saddlebag on a hook to the side of the fireplace, where it dripped ominously. 'I don't hold out much hope for whatever missive is inside that bag,' Philip chuckled to himself.

The messenger settled, Philip turned his attention to the lad's horse. Back in the stable Philip made quick work of removing the horse's tack and saddle, and rubbed the weary mount down. Settling him with some fresh straw and water, and a bag of oats, he was satisfied the horse too would be fine until morning. As he hurried back across to the Abbey buildings Philip had no idea what time it was, but there was no sign of the sun yet. He would go and join his brothers in the cloister. He could pray for that young man, and whatever message he brought. He could pray for Llewellyn now also, with a sincere heart, softened as it was by God's grace and mercy. He had forgiven him, he knew it, and it felt right. 'Thank You, God,' he whispered.

The young man had slept for several hours until disturbed by Brother Aldred and the lay brothers entering the kitchen in order to prepare the simple breakfast permitted for the youngest and oldest of their community. He had eaten with them, a simple meal of bread and honey-drizzled goat's cheese. Only after that had he been able to present his precious missive to the blustering Prior William, who was horrified to find it was personally addressed to the horse master at Abbey Cymer. William relayed this startling information to the abbot, and then held on to the letter for another couple of hours, tempted to break the seal himself. But conscience eventually won out. And so, it was a visibly grumpy William that stood on the threshold of the stable, missive in hand. He could not bring himself to step into the wet muck inside the door, so stood outside. The rain had eased to a heavy mist, but he was still getting rather wet. Hywel glanced up as he heard him approach and stepped over to meet him at the door. William held out the package;

rewrapped in the well-oiled calf skin that had seemingly protected it from the worst of the rain the night before.

'It is for you, brother,' he sniffed. 'It bears Llewellyn's seal and the messenger said it was important.'

Hywel took it from him but made no attempt to open it.

Philip stepped forward out of the gloom of Noble's stall. William's face contorted slightly, disgust registering briefly. Philip couldn't be sure if it was disgust at him personally, or at the smell of the horse muck he now wore on his scapular.

It was evident that the prior was loitering, despite his discomfort, likely hoping to discover for himself the contents of the letter so that he could report back to the abbot. Hywel was not pandering to him. It was surprising that the letter was addressed to Hywel and not to the abbot, but Philip assumed that it was because it was merely concerned with horse matters. He knew how much the prince respected Hywel's expertise. He tried to divert William's attention.

'And the messenger, is he recovered this morning?'

'He is well rested, brother, and thanks you for your care of him and his horse,' William forced the words out. 'He is set to leave when the weather clears a bit more, which it promises to do. He said that Prince Llewellyn does not expect a reply?' The last was more a question, his eyes dropping again to the package in Hywel's hands.

'It is much drier in the stable. Won't you step inside?' Hywel asked him.

The look on William's face was now definitely one of disgust. Even his rampant curiosity would not persuade him to dirty his feet by stepping inside the foul-smelling stable building.

'No, no. The abbot has need of me. I must be going,' he flustered. 'I trust you will inform Father Abbot of any information that pertains to the Abbey, brother?'

'You can be assured that I will, brother,' Hywel replied, with a slight bow.

With another sniff, William turned on his heel and hurried off back towards the abbot's apartments.

Hywel laughed when he was out of earshot. 'Goodness, that man does make it difficult for me not to tease him!'

Philip grinned. 'You did very well, my friend. You were very self-controlled!'

Hywel turned his attention to the missive, unwrapping the skin to find the folded parchment within; it did indeed bear Llewellyn's seal. Hywel took the knife from his belt and carefully slid it under the seal. Moving so that the daylight from the open doorway gave him enough light to read, he opened the folded parchment. As he did so, a separate, smaller, folded piece fluttered to the floor.

Philip had been leaning nonchalantly against a timber roof support with his arms crossed, but leapt forward to rescue the smaller piece of parchment as it fell, barely catching it before it hit the stinking wet stable floor.

'Well caught, brother!' Hywel smiled. 'That is curious, a letter within a letter? Let's see what this is all about.'

He scanned the main document. Philip held the other in his hand but did not open it.

'It is as I thought,' Hywel said. 'It is concerning the horses. The prince wants to take Gwynt when he next visits the Abbey. He has had to make a trip into Chester, which will take him a sennight or so, and plans to divert here on his way back to Abergwyngregyn, his stronghold in the north. He is also planning to bring me another breeding mare or two, if he can source them while across the border in England.'

'Unusual that he would send such instruction as an urgent message,' Philip replied.

'Yes. But then I don't think the horse matters are what made it so important that this message was sent quickly. Nor why it found its way into my hand and not the abbot's.' Hywel looked steadily at Philip. 'There is news here, my friend, news of your family.' Philip stared back at him. Registering what Hywel was saying took a moment.

'My family? The de Braose family? How? Does Llewellyn know who I am?' He paused; his voice had got more agitated, but Hywel was saying nothing in response. He was still stood quietly, looking at him intently. Philip sensed the seriousness of the moment. He took a deep breath, bracing himself.

'What news, Hywel?'

'Your brother John is dead... I'm sorry, Philip.'

Philip stumbled backwards as if hit full-chested by a crossbow bolt. He hit the wall behind him and slid down onto the pile of straw heaped at its base.

John, dead. How was that possible? He was not an old man, only two years older than Philip himself. He wasn't a soldier or mercenary for hire. He was always so strong, so full of life, never ailing. Philip closed his eyes, and breathed out.

'How? Where?'

'A riding accident it seems, at Bramber, his English property. Llewellyn is sparing with the detail. He just adds the information as a codicil at the end here. The letter in your hand is indicated to be for you.' He nodded to the parchment Philip still held in his clenched fist

'I still don't understand. How does he know I am here? That I am a de Braose?' So many questions rushed through his head.

'I cannot be sure, but I think we must look to your Lady Efa for that.'

Philip looked down at the piece of parchment in his hand. 'It does not bear my name.'

'She does not know your name here. She only knows you as Philip, not Brother Robert. I believe Llewellyn took a chance that I would know who you are. He was curious about Noble, recognising a fine fighting horse when he saw one. I answered his enquiry about him by telling him that Noble had come recently to the Abbey with you, and that you were a former soldier. He must have made the connection between that and what Efa had told him about meeting you here. I think you need to read that letter to answer any other questions you might have.'

Philip glanced down at the letter again, still folded in his hand. He was unsure he wanted to know what it contained. He knew that once read, it was likely that his life, this new life, would change irrevocably. Was he ready for that? And yet he owed it to John, to his memory, at least to read it. He swallowed hard as the grief washed over him. John was gone. John who had been his only true family. The boy he had grown up with, endured much with, lived and laughed with – until they had parted in anger and bitterness. Philip let himself remember. He remembered the good times. He remembered the things that had bound them together as brothers. He remembered John's handsome face and proud bearing. He had been a true de Braose, in looks anyway, tall and broad and dark. He remembered the play fights, the foolhardy games, the risky hunts and wild rides. He remembered the happy times when Marared and Efa had first come to Swansea. He remembered when those happy times ended in betrayal, remembered John's face as he had laughed at Philip's pain. He remembered cursing John as he rode away from Swansea and the life he had known. Remembered continuing to curse him for all the years he chased his own demons across the battlefields of France. He remembered with shame that he had wanted to kill his own brother.

Now John was dead. And Philip realised that the only emotion he felt was pure anguish. Grief that he would never see him again, never be able to tell him that he had forgiven him, never be able to try to reconcile with him. All anger had long disappeared, the root of bitterness, the desire to make John pay for what he had done to him. It had all gone. Philip knew it was because he had forgiven John, in his own heart and before God. The process had started for Philip that day on the riverbank where Hywel had shared his own heart-breaking story. Philip had vowed then and there to pursue God's help in forgiving John. It had not come easy at first, but he had long since come to a place of peace. That wound in his own soul had been healed. So now he could grieve as any loving brother would grieve, and not rejoice over his brother's death. He prayed John was with God and at peace himself.

'Do you want to be alone, Philip?' Hywel had moved over and lowered himself down on to his haunches beside him, his face full of concern.

'No.' Philip brought himself back to the present and the contents of the letter now burning a hole in his hand. He shifted so that he sat more comfortably, and took a deep breath. 'I feel I need the safety of this place, and the comfort of your company as I read this. Would you stay? But don't stop your work on my account.'

Hywel grimaced as he rose gingerly back to his feet. 'I am here for you. I will be in with Noble there.' He nodded at the rear end of the hulking beast, and the mess he had made of his stall, and grabbed the rake leaning against the wall. 'My old bones need to keep moving in this damp weather.' He smiled back at Philip.

Philip turned his full attention to the letter. It was sealed but he did not recognise the seal. He opened it carefully with his finger and began to read.

The missive began, 'This is for the hands of Philip de Braose alone.' The writing was neat and delicately scripted. A woman's hand, perhaps?

Philip, if you are reading this you will know now that I have broken my pledge to you. I have confessed to Llewellyn that you are not dead as was thought, and that I know you to be at Abbey Cymer. You will also now know that John, your brother, long lost to you, is dead. He leaves behind Marared, his widow, and three young sons, the eldest, William, barely eight years old. John died two months ago at the end of the summer. News reached us here within the fortnight of his passing. I was then in agony of soul for some weeks, knowing that you would want to know of his death, but also knowing that I had promised not to reveal your secret. I prayed God would make it clear to me what I must do.

This last week further news reached Llewellyn's court and I believe this to have forced my hand. Marared has already had an offer of marriage, from a Sir William Clifford. Clifford is known to Llewellyn, and he will not oppose the match, and Clifford will take good care of your nephew William's lands in England until he reaches his majority. However, Llewellyn did not want to give the care of the lands in the Gower to Clifford, who is a powerful man in his own right. The prince is aware of the uneasy relationship between himself and the princes of Deheubarth. He wants to do nothing to give them reason to turn against him, and they would not look kindly at a powerful English interloper, if Clifford were allowed to take control of the Gower. They had accepted John as Lord of the Gower, and he believed would support the lands staying in de Braose hands, if an acceptable custodian could be found.

Llewellyn was voicing these concerns in my company, knowing my connection with the de Braose family from years ago. I could no longer hold back. Forgive me, Philip. I told him what I knew. That you were alive and had taken temporary refuge from the world within the confines of the Abbey. I told him how you had spoken of your habit as being a 'disguise', and that I was not sure if you had taken vows, or if you were necessarily determined to live out your life in seclusion.

Llewellyn must have remembered then, seeing my emotion, that there had been an attachment between us all those years ago. His face softened, and he comforted me as a father would. And then he asked me if I would write to you, promising to disguise this letter within a missive of his own to protect your identity, and to ask you to consider this.

Would you consider returning to Swansea and taking responsibility for the territories of the Lordship of Gower, on behalf of your nephew, until he is of an age to inherit? Llewellyn will clear the way with Marared and Clifford for it to happen, and as a de Braose you will have the support of the Welsh Princes. To aid you in your task, he has promised to provide you with a wife of his own choosing. Philip, Llewellyn has chosen me to be that wife, he has offered to give me to you. Llewellyn will expect an answer when he returns to the Abbey for his horse. I will be with him, as the Lady Joan desires my company as she accompanies the prince to Chester. Pray on it, Philip, and ask for God's wisdom and direction. I will accept whatever decision you believe to be right before God. Know, however, that if you decide to accept my hand and return to live your life with me, then you will have fulfilled the deepest longings of my own heart. Efa.

Philip leaned his head back against the wall and closed his eyes. He held on tightly to the letter, his hands shaking with emotion. He felt a wave of pure joy go through him, followed by just as powerful feelings of doubt and uncertainty.

'Philip, is it more bad news?'

Hywel had come to stand over him, concerned, rake still in hand.

'Here,' Philip said, handing him the parchment. Hywel put down the rake and took the letter from him.

'Read it for yourself. I have to think, pray, breathe…' He rose unsteadily to his feet and half-staggered towards the open stable door, leaning himself heavily against the doorpost. Outside, the mist had lifted and spots of weak sunlight were appearing through the clouds, illuminating the puddles of water that dotted the yard. After a few moments Philip glanced back at Hywel, who had paused from his own reading and was looking at Philip, disbelief on his face.

'I know,' Philip said. 'This is unexpected. It is huge. I don't know what to do, Hywel. I don't know how to feel, whether to laugh or cry, or maybe both?'

Hywel came to stand by him in the doorway. He took firm hold of Philip's shoulder, but his words were meant to comfort far more than his touch.

'There is One who knows, dear friend. This wasn't at all unexpected for Him. He knows what decisions you must make, and He will reveal His will to you. Trust in Him, Philip, and not in your own emotions at this time. You know what you must do first?'

'Yes.' Philip took a steadying breath. 'I do.'

He pulled his hood up, less against the weather, more to hide himself, and turned resolutely towards the Abbey church.

Keep trusting in the Lord and do what is right in his

eyes.

Fix your heart on the promises of God and you will

be secure,

feasting on his faithfulness.

Make God the utmost delight and pleasure of your

life,

and he will provide for you what you desire the most.

Give God the right to direct your life,

and as you trust him along the way

you'll find he pulled it off perfectly!

Psalm 37:3-5, TPT

16

Restoration

Six days passed, and Philip had spent as much time as was possible in a side chapel in the church, praying and waiting on God. He still couldn't make sense of anything. He desperately needed to hear clearly from God, and now it seemed God had gone quiet on him. His mind was still in turmoil and his heart was too.

Was life with Efa what God wanted for him? The chance to live out in the world again, to return to a place he loved, to even have a family of his own, perhaps? And all under the protection of Llewellyn himself? Everything he had lost restored to him? It seemed too good to be true.

Didn't God require more of him? Didn't he owe it to God to stay here and serve Him, at least for a while longer? He had been so close to giving Him the rest of his life, thought himself ready to shun the world and take his vows. But now, this? Did he really deserve it? He felt so unworthy of God's goodness to him.

Could he resurrect Philip de Braose, and not resurrect the 'old man'?[12] Was he strong enough in his new faith to stay true to God?

He had no words left for God. He took to kneeling with his head resting on his arm on the altar rail. He didn't want to leave the sacred space, he felt God was there, but he was tired of trying to work it out with words. He knew also that the prince

---

[12] Romans 6:6, NKJV.

and his party would be soon upon them. Efa would return and expect him to have it all worked out. The weight of it all bowed him down. His knee was screaming with discomfort, he had knelt there so long, but he could not leave that place. Not until God spoke to him. He was in that position when Hywel found him.

The monk moved quietly to kneel beside him. Philip lifted his head at the familiar presence. He saw Hywel genuflect and bow his own head in prayer briefly before placing one hand on Philip's shoulder.

'Shall we talk?' he asked gently.

'Well, it seems I have exhausted the conversation with God. It seems He has chosen not to speak to me, so you might as well.'

Hywel stood and reached to help Philip to his feet, which was a slow, painful process. Philip's legs felt numb. Hywel led him over to a bench in the main nave of the church.

'Were you expecting God to speak with an audible voice to tell you what to do?'

'I was hopeful.' Philip sagged onto the bench, leaning forward with his hands clasped between his knees. He was exhausted.

'Unfortunately, He doesn't do that very often,' Hywel said, sitting down next to him. 'He uses many other ways to speak to us instead.'

'The small voice inside of us?' Philip had experienced that.

'Yes, His Spirit into our spirit; the "knowing" is how I like to describe it. But He also uses other things to speak to us: the Holy Scriptures, the words of others, creation, even dreams and visions. You have not heard Him in any of those?'

'No. I don't think so. Nothing seems clear to me.' Philip glanced piteously up at Hywel. The old once-familiar feelings of despair felt threateningly close again.

'Hmm. So, what is your own heart telling you to do?'

Philip breathed out a sigh. 'I'm not sure I can trust my heart. The thought of being with Efa, of having her as my wife, makes my heart full to bursting with joy. Then the thought of leaving here, leaving you, leaving God's service, makes my heart grieve deeply.'

'What is your mind telling you to do?' Hywel probed further, his voice still low and gentle.

'Again, it is in turmoil. On the one hand, it tells me I have been given a second chance to live the life I thought lost to me. How foolish would I be to turn it down, when to do so would offend Llewellyn and break Efa's heart? On the other hand, my mind is full of questions, uncertainties, fear, even. If I left, would I lose what I have found here? Would I be tempted back to my old way of life? Would I lose my connection with God? Would I forget the things I have learned? Would I waste what God has done for me?'

'As I thought.' Hywel paused. 'Let me read you something.'

He pulled a book out of his belt. Philip recognised it at once. It was the Psalter that Hywel had given him to read all those many months ago in the infirmary at Grand Selve. It seemed like a lifetime ago now. Hywel opened it up and began to read:

O LORD, You have searched me and known me.
You know my sitting down and my rising up;
You understand my thought afar off.
You comprehend my path and my lying down,
And are acquainted with all my ways.
For there is not a word on my tongue,
But behold, O LORD, You know it altogether.
You have hedged me behind and before,
And laid Your hand upon me.
Such knowledge is too wonderful for me;
It is high, I cannot attain it.

Where can I go from Your Spirit?
Or where can I flee from Your presence?
If I ascend into heaven, You are there;
If I make my bed in hell, behold, You are there.
If I take the wings of the morning,

And dwell in the uttermost parts of the sea,
Even there Your hand shall lead me,
And Your right hand shall hold me.
If I say, 'Surely the darkness shall fall on me,'
Even the night shall be light about me;
Indeed, the darkness shall not hide from You,
But the night shines as the day;
The darkness and the light are both alike to You.

For You formed my inward parts;
You covered me in my mother's womb.
I will praise You, for I am fearfully and wonderfully made;
Marvelous are Your works,
And that my soul knows very well.
My frame was not hidden from You,
When I was made in secret,
And skillfully wrought in the lowest parts of the earth.
Your eyes saw my substance, being yet unformed.
And in Your book they all were written,
The days fashioned for me,
When as yet there were none of them.[13]

Philip sat up as Hywel began to read, and listened intently. He felt the peace of God descend on them both as the words washed over him.

Hywel paused in his reading. 'Can you hear God now?' He looked over at Philip.

'The words you are reading are for me, aren't they?'

'I believe so, yes. What does it say to you?'

'That God knows everything about me, has known me since I was in my mother's womb, knew what my life would be like from the beginning, knows how it will go from here on. He knows what I am about to speak even before I speak it, let alone what the next step is that I should take. And His hedge of protection is always around me.'

---

[13] Psalm 139:1-16, NKJV.

'Yes. And?' Hywel smiled encouragingly.

'That bit in the middle. I think He is saying that wherever I go, He will be with me. He will be as much with me in the Gower as He has been with me here. I will always be able to find Him. He will never leave me to my own devices, His hand is heavy on my life. He will always be there to lead, guide and protect me.'

Hywel let him ponder those things for a few moments, before speaking again.

'Philip, you cling to the life here because it feels safe. You have known peace here, and you have grown closer to God here, and in some ways that has been very good. But where were you when God first encountered you?'

Philip paused to recall before answering. 'God sent you to me when I was lying in a roadside ditch.'

'Yes, and then, where were you when you returned your heart to Him?'

'In a pig shed!' Philip laughed briefly at the memory.

'And how many of the lessons that you have learned – the things I have shared with you, the people who have influenced you – have happened outside these Abbey walls?'

'I get your point.' Philip smiled wryly.

'I think you have to consider, Philip, whether it is only fear stopping you from taking what God is offering you, and grasping it with both hands. If it is fear, then you need to just step through it. I believe that you will find, if you do, that what you feared most was merely an illusion.'

'He wants me to have it all, doesn't He?' The realisation of that truth was beginning to sink in. 'God wants me to be happy, to be loved, to be fulfilled, to be useful. For me that could be as a husband, a custodian, a father, even. I still can't quite believe it, that this is the reason He restored my life. I wanted to believe there was some great act of service I was to do for Him, some noble sacrifice on my part, a life of devotion to Him to pay Him back for what He has done for me.'

'You can still live a life of devotion to Him, brother, out there in the world. You can still serve Him in serving others. In telling your story, you can instil hope in the hopeless. In loving others as you have been loved, they too can experience the love of God. Caring for the poor and needy, sharing your life and sharing your faith – you don't need an abbey church, or a cloister, or a monk's habit to do those things. Nor do you need prayer offices, and rules and vows. I think, Philip, you are called to live a different life from us here. But a life as much devoted to God as ours is.'

'I think perhaps you are right.' Philip smiled again. 'It seems you are right a great deal of the time!'

Hywel snorted. 'If only *that* were right, brother!'

Philip sat in the joy and peace of the moment. He had his answer, he could make his decision and it felt right. A cry of praise rose up in his heart to God. Then another thought clouded his mind and filled him with sudden dread.

'How?' He turned back to Hywel who seemed to be enjoying his own peaceful moment, sitting with his eyes closed, hands relaxed in his lap.

'How?' Hywel opened his eyes reluctantly.

'Yes, *how*? How do I leave here? I can't just get up and go. That would be cruel, unkind and ungracious. I have friends here now. I owe the community so much. Even the abbot and Prior William. I have to leave well. I have to leave so that I can return in good relationship. I need to be able to come back to visit – to visit you. And I can't tell them the truth,' he continued, his voice cracking slightly. 'If it were to come out that you had conspired with me in this deception, you would be disgraced. And those who abetted you – Jerome, Julian – also disgraced. I could not live with that on my conscience.' He looked pleadingly at Hywel, who just closed his eyes and resumed his relaxed position.

'You must do what you feel is right.' He seemed strangely unconcerned.

'I pray, then, that God will guide me in what to do,' Philip said, eventually.

'My friend, I believe He will.' Hywel added. 'I believe God will give you the right words to say in this situation. He promises us Holy Spirit wisdom when we ask for it.[14] In fact, He is wisdom itself, and you, my brother, are wiser than you give yourself credit for. Between you and God, I trust that you will know what to do, when the time is right to do it. God will go before you and will be with you, and He will be in you.'

That time came soon enough. The following day, around noon, the clatter of horses' hooves on the bridge announced Llewellyn's arrival. He arrived unannounced, which threw Prior William into a panic. It was a normal day for the community, so there was no provision for guests to eat anything other than the simple fare the monks normally ate. They had no fish or meat to offer the prince and his retinue. William came out bowing low and fussing around the prince, who had pulled up outside the Abbey gate, but not dismounted.

'My lord!' His already high-pitched voice had gone up another pitch or two with agitation. 'We had no word you would be here today. We knew you would come at some time, Brother Hywel informed us of that, but if we had known that you would come today we would have made provision for you. I cannot expect you to sit and eat our simple fare. The abbot will be mortified that he cannot set a fine table for you and your...' He paused mid-sentence, surprise evident on his face. Llewellyn had only two armed men and two ladies with him. The prince was sitting, relaxed, on his horse, looking bemused at the monk's discomfort.

'Fret not, brother. We will not inconvenience you today. As you can see, I am travelling light. I have left the majority of my retinue at an inn in nearby Dolgellau. They have fed us well there already. We came only to do some horse dealings, and will

---

[14] James 1:5.

not keep you from your prayers. I presume the horse master is with the horses now?' Llewellyn turned his horse without waiting for an answer, as if to dismiss the monk who was still hovering, jumping from one foot to the other.

'If you are sure. Will you at least stop to have a cup of wine with the abbot? We – I mean, he – would be sorry to not offer you that much as a gesture of hospitality.'

Llewellyn grunted. 'After we have done what we came for, perhaps. Now if you will excuse us, brother.' He spurred his horse into a trot before the prior could say more. The party left William standing there with a look of consternation on his face, as they led their horses around the side of the church to the stables beyond.

Following Sext, Philip had gone with Hywel to exercise the horses in the yard. They always walked Noble first to minimise his interaction with the other horses, and Philip was just leading him back towards the stable when the sound of approaching riders made him pause. He tied the old horse loosely to a fencepost, and Hywel came over to join him. The five riders reined to a halt just inside the stable yard and Llewellyn and his retainers dismounted. Hywel moved to greet the prince. Philip was drawn instead to a fine grey horse, whose reins he took in his hands. Not Llewellyn's horse, but Efa's. He glanced up to find her looking at him, her face wary. Her eyes probed his, and he responded with a small smile and a single nod of his head. She responded with a blush to her cheeks, but her eyes lit up with something that looked much like relief.

Llewellyn spoke. 'So this is him, then?'

Philip took a step back, releasing Efa's horse, and turned to face Llewellyn. Llewellyn made an imposing figure as he stood tall before him. Philip bowed slightly as a sign of respect, but stood unflinching as the prince inspected him.

'Yes, I can see it now, he has something of the de Braose look about him. Not as ugly as his grandfather, mind; he should be thankful for that.' He was walking slowly around Philip, assessing him like he might a prize stallion. 'I remember him as a scrawny lad. This man is not that. A fighter, by the looks of him. Not big, but strong enough.'

'I can handle a weapon, my lord.' Philip refused to be cowed, but did not want to be disrespectful either. He was a de Braose, after all, if a changed one. 'I hope never to have to lift a sword in anger again, but I can defend myself, and those I am called to protect.'

'Hmm. I don't doubt that you could. So, Philip, you are not dead, just hiding, eh?' Llewellyn looked keenly at him, unsmiling.

'Some might call it that, my lord. I call it finding the man I was designed by God to be. I am not the Philip de Braose I was. Not in looks, and not in character, thanks be to God. But some things have not changed.' Philip paused. 'I still care about my family, I still miss the Gower lands, and I still love this lady.' He glanced up at Efa, who blushed again and dipped her head demurely.

'So you will agree to my proposition, then? You will return to life outside the Church, to the Gower, to serve your family, for my grandson's sake?' the prince continued.

'I will. If you keep your side of the bargain?' A little challenge felt called for.

'Huff. You mean the lady here? Well, unless I get a better offer for her!'

Efa let out a small cry at that, and Philip looked up to see her glaring at Llewellyn. The horse bearing Lady Joan stepped forward. 'Llewellyn!' She spoke softly, but there was a warning note in her voice.

'Ha!' The prince bellowed. 'Stand down, ladies. I was only jesting!' He was grinning broadly now, but it was impossible to really know if he had been jesting or not. He turned his attention back to Philip. 'We are staying at a local inn tonight, but will be back here at first light. You'd best be ready. I assume you are bringing that great beast with you? Looks ready to retire to me.' He nodded at Noble.

Noble snorted in disgust. Philip stepped over to grab his bridle. He didn't quite trust the horse not to make a charge at the prince, to prove just how fit he still was.

'Yes, Noble will be coming with us. But like me, his fighting days are over. Will we,' he glanced up at Efa, 'be heading straight for the Gower?'

'No. I plan for you to wed at Abergwyngregyn, in full sight of everyone, so that no one will question your right to the position I have asked you to take. Or your right to marry Efa.'

It was a statement, not a question. But Philip was content. Efa deserved a wedding celebration, and Llewellyn's blessing would definitely protect them both.

'*I* am convinced enough that you are de Braose, but what if you are questioned by others?' Llewellyn asked him. Philip reached beneath his scapula and produced his dagger. He handed it hilt first to Llewellyn, who examined it admiringly.

'Ah, yes, a quality blade and a clear family inscription, I see. I will give you a seal of my own to carry on your person too. That should suffice.' He handed the knife back to Philip, who returned it to his belt.

'Now, Hywel, where's this young horse of mine?' Llewellyn was obviously keen to move on to other things. 'The two mares the ladies are riding are the horses we brought back from Chester for your approval. If you want them, I can leave both of them here when we pass through tomorrow morning. The ladies wanted to ride them today but they have other mounts back with my party at Dolgellau that they can use to ride north, if you want to keep these. I think, however, that the Lady Efa has already grown attached to the grey. She sits well on her.'

Hywel walked around Efa's horse, throwing the lady a grin and a wink. 'Hmm. She is bigger than what I was looking for,' he said, trying to keep his tone serious. 'The Lady Joan's steed, though…' he turned to the other horse, 'a fine blue roan, with a jet black mane, now, she is sweet. She would make a great addition to the breeding stock here.'

Llewellyn laughed and clapped his hand on Hywel's shoulder as they walked over to where the other horses stood idly waiting at the other end of the yard, their exercise so rudely interrupted. Lady Joan dismounted and wandered after her husband, leaving Philip with Efa. He stepped forward to her horse again, but she stayed mounted to keep a respectful distance between them. They were aware of the potential of eyes on them from windows above.

'Thank you,' he whispered, as he pretended to adjust the horse's bridle. His hands were trembling.

'For what?' She was smiling down at him.

'Everything. The letter, breaking your vow… wanting me.'

'You won't regret leaving here for me?' A note of concern etched her voice.

'No. No more regrets. Only hope.' He glanced back up at her. He stroked the horse's neck to prevent his hands from reaching out to grasp hers.

'Tomorrow, my love, tomorrow,' she whispered, her voice full, as Llewellyn and Hywel strode back to join them.

'Yes, we'll take Gwynt with us tomorrow, and leave the roan with you,' the prince was saying. He reached Philip and Efa, and stopped in front of Philip again. He bowed once, a formal greeting.

'Philip de Braose, I presume?' He looked intently at Philip. It was one last challenge.

'My lord Prince, at your service.' Philip bowed in response.

Philip stood outside the heavy wooden door and prayed one last prayer. A plea for help. Standing under Llewellyn's scrutiny earlier had been hard enough. He dreaded this next confrontation even more so, but it had to be done. He knocked once and the face of Prior William appeared around the door.

'Brother Robert?' William eyed him suspiciously.

'I would speak with Father Abbot, if it is convenient?' Philip replied respectfully. He would not let William rile him tonight.

The door shut, not quite with a slam, but almost. A few minutes passed before it opened again, wide, and Prior William stood back to let him in.

'You may leave us, Prior.' The abbot was seated on his chair by the table. A small fire burned in the hearth, but the room still felt chilled. William did not seem keen to leave, walking painfully slowly towards the door, and glancing back more than once. The abbot appeared resolute, however, and the monk got the message and reluctantly left the room.

Only after the prior had gone did Abbot Thomas address Philip. 'Come, sit close, so that I can see your face. I can hear you then without you having to shout. No one else needs to overhear what you have come to say.' He nodded to the door that William had just closed behind him.

Philip sat in a chair at the table, turning it slightly so that he faced the abbot.

'I have been watching you.'

Philip looked up in surprise. He had bowed his head to gather his thoughts before speaking, but the abbot had spoken first.

'People think that because I am old and deaf, and nearly blind, that I don't see things. But I observe more than they think. I see William's ambition, I see Pedr's devotion, and I see that you are not settled here.'

'But…' Philip started to interrupt, to perhaps defend himself in some way, but the abbot held up his hand to silence him.

'You have done nothing wrong. You have done all that I could have asked and more, to make yourself a part of our community. You have worked hard, and done so with a willing heart and a ready smile. You have been pious in your religious observance. No one has a bad word to say about you. Even William could not help admiring your illuminations; I think even he is warming a little towards you. No, you have made a home for yourself among us. But I think it is not enough for you. Am I right?'

'You have great insight, Father Abbot. What has made you question my vocation?'

'I have been a Cistercian for a very long time, my son. I have seen very many brothers come and go. Men have many reasons for entering this life. Some feel called by God, some come owing to an accident of birth; a second or subsequent son destined for the Church. Some come later in life for a peaceful retirement from the world, some come attracted by community life, and some come just to escape.' He looked at Philip pointedly, before continuing. 'They have their reasons for coming, and they also have their reasons for staying. Aldred stays because he has already known another life, Pedr stays because he wants no other life. I perceive that you have lived another life, and while you do not want to go back to that life, you wonder if the life here is enough for you. Am I right that you came late to your calling?'

'Yes, I did.' It was no lie. He tensed, waiting for further interrogation.

'Brother Robert...' The abbot paused on his name. 'I do not need to know where you came from, or who you are.'

Philip relaxed.

'But you want to leave us?' The abbot asked him straight.

'Yes, Father Abbot... and no,' Philip sighed. 'It's not that I *want* to leave. I have felt at home here. I love the life here, the Abbey, my brothers. I have been welcomed and accepted, and found purpose and peace here.' He paused to find the right words. 'It is rather that now I believe God is calling me to walk a different path.'

'As a husband and father, perhaps?'

Philip took a sharp intake of breath. Did he know? Had the abbot seen him with Efa?

The abbot smiled then. 'Do not be alarmed. I am merely guessing, although your reaction gives you away.'

'Yes, forgive me, Father Abbot. I love a woman once lost to me. I entered this life believing she was lost to me forever. Now it seems God has brought her back to me. I thought I owed

God my whole life, and that that meant inside these Abbey walls. I have come to see that devotion to God, a lifetime of devotion to Him, can take many forms, not all requiring separation from the world.'

The abbot thought on his words, nodding his understanding.

'Again, I won't ask how this all came about.' The abbot looked directly at him. 'Although I suppose Hywel is involved in it somehow.' His lips twitched as if he were trying not to smile. 'Brother Robert,' he said, 'you have my blessing to leave us. You won't be the first, and you won't be the last to turn their back on this life. You do know, however, how serious it is to break your vows?'

Philip looked away. What could he say in response that would not expose himself, and Hywel? Then suddenly something he had read earlier in the day came to mind.

'*Offer to God thanksgiving, And pay your vows to the Most High.*'

'Psalm 50?' The abbot nodded appreciatively.

'Yes, Father. It goes on to say, *"Whoever offers praise glorifies Me; And to him who orders his conduct aright I will show the salvation of God"*.[15] I understand that to mean that God does not want empty, meaningless offerings made out of compulsion; rather, He wants hearts of thanksgiving and praise, and lives lived righteously. If we live this way, we are truly fulfilling our vows to Him. Whether within abbey walls or not.' Philip sat back nervously. Was it impertinent to be explaining to the abbot what he thought Scripture said?

The abbot looked at him thoughtfully. 'Wise words, my son, wise words. I have great hope for you. God go with you and help you to fulfil those very vows.' He lifted his hand in a blessing and then nodded towards the door.

'News of your departure will spread fast. I encourage you to take your leave well. Speak to every one of your brothers privately. You need give them no more explanation than you have given me. Some will question more. I caution you to say

---

[15] Psalm 50:14, 23, NKJV.

only what is necessary. Most will wish you well. All will miss you, I am sure.'

'Thank you, Father.' Philip stood. The abbot stretched out his hand and Philip bowed and kissed it before taking his leave.

Lord, you know everything there is to know about me.

You perceive every movement of my heart and soul, and you understand my every thought before it even enters my mind.

You are so intimately aware of me, Lord.

You read my heart like an open book and you know all the words I'm about to speak before I even start a sentence!

You know every step I will take before my journey even begins.

You've gone into my future to prepare the way, and in kindness you follow behind me to spare me from the harm of my past.

With your hand of love upon my life, you impart a blessing to me.

This is just too wonderful, deep, and

incomprehensible!

Psalm 139:1-6, TPT

Epilogue

Philip had taken the abbot's advice and every one of the brothers at Cymer had been kind enough to wish him well. Some were more understanding than others. But it was with a light heart that Philip rode away from Cymer that autumn morning, made yet lighter by the sight of his beloved on her grey horse, and the realisation of the joy that lay ahead of them.

Leaving Hywel had been the hardest, but the monk never lost his smile as he embraced Philip and clapped him firmly on the back, almost knocking the wind from his lungs.

'This is not goodbye, my friend. I'll find reason to visit you, and I expect to see you back here. Don't let sadness mar this day for you, Philip; rejoice in all that God has done for you, as I rejoice to have been allowed to be a part of it. I have watched God work a miracle of restoration in your life, and I have done all that He asked of me to help you in that process. I am proud of you, and so thankful to God.'

He was still beaming as usual, but Philip had detected a moistness in those familiar eyes.

'I will never forget you, or your stories, or our journey together. I am a better man for knowing you, and I will be eternally grateful to God for that.' Philip had embraced him back.

'Enough!' Hywel had pushed him playfully away. 'Get up on that horse and get away. Your new wife and your new life awaits you!'

It wasn't the last time they saw each other. Hywel visited Swansea more than once, on the pretence of horse matters, and Philip and Efa often found reason to stop off at Cymer, when heading north. The last time the two of them visited Hywel, he was dying. He was still an impressive man, but his eyes were dim, his hands gnarled with age, and he could no longer care for his beloved horses. Once that was no longer possible, it seemed as if Hywel yearned even more for the life to come, and having said one more farewell to his friends that night, he slipped peacefully away. Abbot Pedr sang the sweetest of songs as they lowered Hywel's remains into the soil at Cymer, and Philip rejoiced that now his friend would be singing sweetly himself, before the very throne of God, in perfect harmony with the angels and saints.

Efa and Philip built a happy life for themselves in Swansea, blessed, if not completely free of heartache. They waited a painfully long time to be parents. The longed-for child was a girl. They named her Carys, meaning 'beloved', to celebrate the love that had brought her into being. She was a complete joy to them, and grew into a fine, God-fearing young woman. They cautioned her to be careful with her heart, but were blessed when she chose to marry a man of good character, and for love alone.

Efa and Philip kept their pledge to Llewellyn, long after the great prince himself was no more. They stewarded the Gower lands well for their nephew William, until he was of an age to take them on, and then they were given the small castle at Pennard, where they lived out their lives together. Philip never lost his devotion to God, despite his fear to the contrary. He kept his own rhythm of prayer, setting aside times every day to be with God, however busy his life became. He never forgot the strength he had found in the life of prayer taught him by the Cistercians. Gratefulness for the blessings God had gifted them with spurred them on to give the very best of themselves back to Him, and to those He put in their lives. He gave them both very many opportunities to serve the needs of others, and share their stories and their faith.

Efa left Philip suddenly, early one spring morning; he woke to find her gone. He lay holding her hand, weeping, but joyful that she was with God and at peace. He felt the sting of loneliness then, and despair once more knocked on the door of his heart. Hywel was gone, Carys had her own life and family, and Noble had passed on at a ripe old age. And now, too, his beloved wife. But Philip knew how to find peace again. He rose one morning, saddled his horse and heaved his tired bones up into the saddle, that knee still reminding him of the injury that had changed his life direction all those years before. He made the long journey north to Cymer, stopping off on the way to bless those he could, remembering how Hywel had taught him to listen and respond to God's promptings.

He was greeted at Cymer like the old friend he was. Abbot Pedr led him to his own rooms and insisted on him having his own bed to rest on. Philip himself insisted on one more visit to the Abbey church, where he sat and listened to the brothers singing plainsong, and to the familiar words of the liturgy. He sat in the place where he had spoken with God so many times before, and felt again the closeness of His presence. Filled again with God's peace, he made his way back to Pedr's room and lay wearily down on the bed. He closed his eyes, and asked God if he could leave this life now. It was not a wish to die born out of despair, as it had been all those years before. No, this time it was just his heart's overwhelming desire to be with God for ever.

God answered his prayer that night, and Philip de Braose passed peacefully from death to life eternal, his healing complete.

O Israel, hope in the LORD;

For with the LORD *there is mercy,*

And with Him is abundant redemption.

Psalm 130:7, NKJV (emphasis mine)

I am the Lord who heals *you (Jehovah Rapha).*

Exodus 15:26, NKJV (emphasis and brackets mine)

Acknowledgements

Thank you to the lovely people at Instant Apostle for believing in *The Healing*, and for your commitment to getting the best possible finished product. Your patience, grace and professionalism in everything made the publishing process a delight. Thank you.

Thank you to my family whose love for me has given me a secure place to live and grow in. To my husband, Tim, for staying by my side through everything. Thank you for your unwavering support and encouragement, and for your understanding when the writing took over our lives in ways we didn't quite anticipate. To my children Keren and Peter. I am so thankful to God for you two. You have been, and continue to be, my constant joy and inspiration. To Jacob and Baby M, you just add to that joy! And to my wider family – thank you for just being you. I love you all.

Thank you to my church family, for standing with us and enfolding us with your love. Thank you for every prayer prayed and every word of encouragement spoken. Your words are all over this book. Special thanks to Lynn and Alick Ford. In the same way as Brother Hywel was used to rescue Philip, God used you two to help rescue me. This book simply would not exist without you. I am eternally grateful to God for you both, in ways I can't even express, and I love you dearly.

Thank you to my many friends, near and far, old and new. Your friendships have helped shape me, and your continued love and support blesses me more than I can say.

Above all, thank you God, my healer and redeemer, and the lover of my soul. It is all from You and all for You.